"Hoku, Navigator, Medusa, and Joker, and all the wild horses were swimming in that filthy water," she whispered to Ann.

"Darby." Ann said her name pointedly, as if she'd missed something obvious.

"What?" she asked.

"You were swimming in it." Ann frowned.

Darby's mouth tasted sour as she recalled her fall from Hoku that same day. She'd taken in a gulp of that awful water that one of the firefighters had called junk soup.

Darby pulled up the neck of her pink polo shirt to cover her lips.

"Too late," Ann told her, and though she was smiling, her eyes looked worried.

Check out the

Phantom Stallion

series, also by Terri Farley!

Read all of Darby's adventures!

Phantom Stallion
WILD HORSE ISLAND

Phantom Stallion

WILD HORSE ISLAND 8

WATER LILY

TERRI FARLEY

HarperTrophy®
An Imprint of HarperCollinsPublishers

Disclaimer

Wild Horse Island is imaginary. Its history, legends, people, and ecology echo Hawaii's, but my stories and reality are like leaves on the rain-forest floor. They may overlap, but their edges never really match.

Water Lily
Copyright © 2008 by Terri Sprenger-Farley

Library of Congress Catalog Card Number: 2007942468
ISBN 978-0-06-088621-9

❖

First Harper Trophy edition, 2008

To Dianne and Ted Nelson and their amazing staff and volunteers—especially Patti and Palomino—for making the Wild Horse Sanctuary in Shingletown, California, the home of the real Phantom . . .

To Bonnie Matton and the Wild Horse Preservation League for putting their heads where their hearts are . . .

And to Lacy J. Dalton, whose songs lift up wild horses and the West. We're all with you when you sing, "Let 'em run!"

© Gary Chalk

TWO SISTERS VOLCANOES

MESSAGE
BOTTLE LANDING

IOLANI
RANCH

RAIN
FOREST

SUN
HOUSE

OLD PLANTATION

TUTU'S
COTTAGE

CRIMSON
VALE

NIGHT DIGGER
POINT BEACH

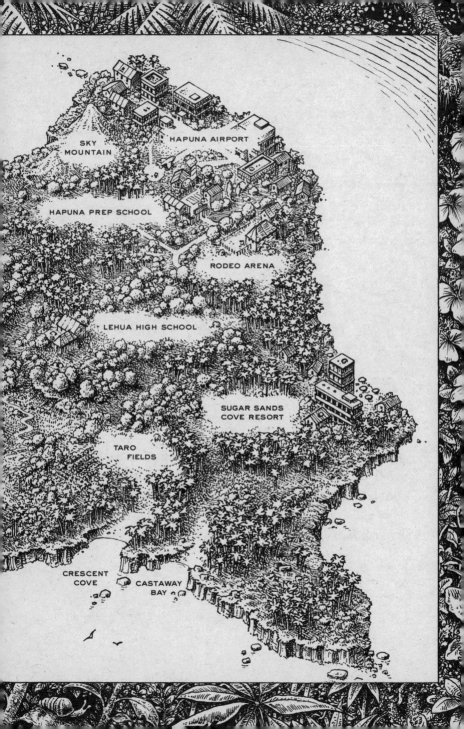

 Chapter One

Darby Carter lay belly down, as level to the ground as she could make herself. Her chin rested on red dirt. The grass of the Lehua High School football field tickled her nose, but everything about her remained still.

Except for her eyes.

They tracked the wild horses' steps as they followed the early-morning sun.

Without raising her head, Darby could only see the black stallion from hooves to chest. He stood that close.

Darby's best friend, Ann Potter, lay beside her. Ann was supposed to be equally still and silent. Though her unruly red curls didn't move, Ann whispered an imitation of a documentary film narrator.

"While stalking the crafty colts of Wild Horse Island—"

"Shh." Darby tried not to smile.

"—two intrepid naturalists were unable to conceal themselves from a pack of slobbering sophomores, with the end result that they were trampled quite—"

"Ann!" Darby scolded. She elbowed her friend in the ribs, even though the black mustang hadn't bolted.

They weren't stalking crafty colts, or concealing themselves from other students—sophomores or otherwise—but after two frustrating weeks, she and Ann had given up following the rules.

Fearing the stallion would charge some student, the parents, teachers, Department of Agriculture, and the school's principal, Ms. Cooke, had all been taking turns patrolling the horses' temporary pasture at the school to keep the kids away.

They've been pretty good at it, too, Darby thought. Each time she and Ann had come out to the field to check on the wild horses they'd helped rescue from the tsunami, they were shooed away "for their own safety."

This morning they'd finally crept close enough to really watch the horses, because they'd persuaded Ann's dad to drop them off an hour before classes began.

Darby had expected it to be cold this early in the day, but it hadn't rained since the tsunami. The earth was drying out and felt almost warm beneath her. Sunshine heated the denim of her jeans, too, but Darby didn't close her eyes and bask.

Who knew when she'd get this close to the horses

again? She took in every detail of Black Lava, studying the sloping pasterns and wispy feathers on the black stallion's legs.

He could run forever, Darby thought. She sighed, and the stallion lowered his head to investigate the sound. Equine eyes—one brown and one blue as her own—fixed on her.

"He's watching us." At Ann's voice, a bay mare gave a low nicker and moved farther away.

Nine horses remained in Black Lava's band. Before the tsunami, there'd been eleven.

Snorting, the night-black stallion moved far enough away that Darby saw all of him. Head high, he trotted a circle around his herd. He seemed to count each of them—the bay mare and her black foal, a yellow dun with matching foal, a gray mare with a blue roan foal, and a putty-colored dun, chestnut, and black mare standing off to one side.

The stallion stopped beside the dun mare and lifted his muzzle as if pointing out the girls. He stood half a football field away, but Darby heard wind sing through his tail.

He and the dun sniffed, nostrils widened to take in the smell of the humans.

The horses had been forced to call this place home, but they didn't welcome visitors.

A squeal from one of the mares sent the herd off at a run, to the far side of the field. What had startled them?

Before Darby could roll up on her side to investigate, a voice told her it was a *who*, not a *what*.

"You don't mind standing up and coming with me,
do you?"

Darby closed her eyes. She knew they were caught
but didn't want to face it.

"Girls?"

Darby and Ann pushed themselves onto their knees,
then stood, brushing at the grass and dirt on their
clothes as they looked at each other and tried to think of
something to say.

"No surf this morning?" Ann asked finally.

"I could find bigger waves in my bathtub," the
principal said.

Ms. Cooke was a world-class surfer. Most mornings she arrived at school with her sun-bleached hair
still wet. But the moment she stashed her teal-blue
surfboard behind her office door, Ms. Cooke turned
into a no-nonsense principal.

"Let's go." Ms. Cooke strode off.

She clearly expected them to follow, and though
excuses swirled through Darby's mind, she couldn't
find the nerve to say anything. She'd seen Ms. Cooke
around campus, but they'd never met.

Ann was less intimidated by the principal. As the
girls caught up with her, Ann pointed in the opposite
direction. "Our first class is this way, Ms. Cooke."

Ms. Cooke's smile crinkled the skin around her
eyes. "We're headed for the office. You two knew the

field was off-limits. You took a chance and lost."

"What's going to happen?" Darby knew she sounded chicken.

"A citation," Ms. Cooke's voice floated back to them as she continued walking. "And Nutrition Break detention for the rest of the week."

"A citation?" Darby gasped.

That was bad. Really bad. Short term, it might mean she couldn't ride out with her friend Cade to Crimson Vale today after school. Long term, it could be a disaster.

One of her mother's ground rules for remaining in Hawaii and on 'Iolani Ranch with her grandfather was: Darby must earn good grades. Of course that meant citizenship grades, too. Her mother said perfect behavior didn't take much brainpower.

Although Darby had been in Hawaii for only two and a half months, she'd already been in trouble more than she had during her entire life in Southern California.

Megan Kato, the daughter of the business manager on 'Iolani Ranch and one of Darby's best friends, had told Darby it was because she was actually doing things— riding the grasslands of wild Hawaii, for a start—instead of sitting in her room reading.

Darby had used that explanation when her mother, Ellen Kealoha Carter, had visited last week. An actress, Ellen was shooting a pilot for a TV series in Tahiti. Early reviews of the new series were great, and Ellen had said that since her time would be divided between Southern California and Tahiti, Darby's plea that the two of them live in Hawaii was a possibility.

Since Ellen had grown up on Wild Horse Island, she'd been somewhat understanding about Darby's adventures and mishaps.

But no excuse would do if a formal reprimand was placed in Darby's school file.

Darby's mind raced, searching for some way out of this. She concentrated on her honey-brown boots. They moved in step with Ann's blue-gray ones as they crossed the campus behind the principal. Curious looks and a few laughs followed them.

She must have swallowed audibly as she got ready to negotiate with Ms. Cooke, because Ann gave a quick shake of her head. Her expression said things could be a lot worse, so Darby didn't protest. She just hurried to keep up.

The bell for first period was ringing when Darby and Ann finished signing their names to forms detailing their punishment. The girls were sprinting, hoping to get to class on time when Megan Kato waved her hand and shouted to get their attention from across the hall.

"Hey! You get to see the horses?"

"We did, but oh my gosh, Meggie, you'll never guess what kind of trouble—"

Darby tugged at Ann's sleeve. Ann and Megan had been soccer teammates and were friends. If Ann stopped to explain, in her usual dramatic detail, they'd be tardy to English.

"We'll tell you at lunch, okay?" Darby said.

"Keep letting Crusher get you in trouble, and you'll make me look like the angel of the family," Megan said. She formed her fingers in a halo above her cherry-Coke-colored hair before hurrying toward her own class.

Darby hitched her backpack up higher and vowed she wouldn't let Megan's prediction come true.

After English and History, Ann and Darby pulled off their sweatshirts, glad to be rid of them as the day heated up, and trudged back to the office.

Darby's stomach growled as they passed one of the snack carts that rolled out during Nutrition Break.

"Will we just have to sit in the office until break is over?" Darby asked.

Ann should know. Since the soccer accident that had broken her kneecap, she'd worked in the office instead of having P.E.

"No, Ms. Cooke will think of something productive for us to do," Ann said.

"Like clear this crowd?" Darby said as they tried to get into the office building.

Ann and Darby squeezed through the doorway past a line of students snaking out of the nurse's office.

"I've got to go home," said a girl hunched over the attendance counter.

"Can you call my mom?" asked a boy slumped in a counselor's office doorway.

"What's going on?" Ann sidestepped a girl seated on the office floor.

Wrapped in a white sweater and shivering even though it had to be eighty degrees outside, the girl moaned, "I'm going to be sick!"

Her shaky voice lent the claim enough credibility that Ann and Darby gave her some space.

"There's Ms. Cooke," Ann said.

The principal and her secretary both held phones. They were both talking, but Ms. Cooke still spotted them. She nodded toward the office door as if they should leave.

No way, Darby thought, remembering the form she'd signed. Maybe Ms. Cooke had forgotten but Darby hadn't, and she didn't want to get into even worse trouble by skipping her punishment.

"We're supposed to have detention," Darby reminded the principal. She said it quietly, not wanting to announce her disgrace to the entire school.

The principal must have heard, because she swung the receiver away from her mouth without moving the earpiece. "Wiki wiki," she said, waving them toward the exit again.

"That means 'hurry up'—" Ann said.

The principal, talking right over her, added, "You don't want to get sick, too."

"Okay." Ann grabbed Darby's elbow, even though

she wasn't lagging behind.

The principal's insistence convinced them to move so quickly, they were actually early for their next class.

"Mr. Silva, I think we've got a plague," Ann told their Ecology teacher as she slammed her books down on her desk.

"A plague?" Mr. Silva rubbed his hands together in anticipation.

"No, really," Ann said.

Darby smiled. Mr. Silva's billowing white lab coat, long, gray-streaked black hair, and passion for science set him apart from other teachers at Lehua High School. He was definitely one of her favorites.

As Ann described the scene in the office, more students came in and the bell rang, but Mr. Silva still listened intently, tapping an index finger against his lips. Then he asked Ann to tell the class what she and Darby had seen in the office.

"Students," Mr. Silva said, once Ann stopped for breath. "What sorts of environmental complications from a tsunami might cause illness?"

"Mosquitoes!"

"Mud!"

Mr. Silva wrote each suggestion on the white board with a red marker.

"Rashes!"

"Malaria!"

The first thing to pop into Darby's mind was gross,

but Mr. Silva created such an open atmosphere, she said it anyway.

"Corpses!"

Everyone turned to look at her. Most of the hands that were raised faltered, then fell, but Mr. Silva wrote it on the white board with the others.

"Man," said a disgusted voice. "Corpses?"

Few students turned around. Everyone knew the perpetually scornful voice came from the guy in a hooded gray sweatshirt who sat in the back of the room.

". . . such a jerk," someone muttered.

Darby knew she should ignore Tyson, knew she shouldn't care that he didn't like her, but curiosity won out over logic.

She couldn't help looking over her shoulder to search his face for some clue as to *why* he disliked her, why, when he did lower himself to talk with her, it was to say something rude. Just a couple weeks ago he'd called her a haole crab.

"What's wrong with corpses?" Darby said, and then everyone laughed and she felt her face go hot with a blush. "I mean"—she turned to face Mr. Silva—"don't they pollute the water?"

"They don't improve it, certainly," Mr. Silva said, and that made Darby laugh, too. "And though corpses are a concern in cases of tuberculosis and cholera, they rarely cause epidemics."

"Like there even were corpses," Tyson grumbled.

"I saw some. Floating! A horse, some pigs—"

Darby broke off when other students chimed in with their own sightings of dead birds, mongooses, and giant moths.

With a nod, as if they'd pretty much covered that topic, Mr. Silva circled back to mud.

Students groaned when he talked about tsunami victims in Asia who'd had mud drained from their lungs or had wounds scoured open to clean out contamination from mud.

"So, what about all the sick people in the office?" Ann asked.

"Malaria and West Nile virus don't usually come until six to eight weeks after flooding," Mr. Silva explained.

"So, it's probably like, mass hysteria," scoffed Tyson.

"That's possible," Mr. Silva said. "But my bet's on pollutants getting into the water supply through cracked pipes." Mr. Silva's voice grew excited as he reached for a shallow glass container on a shelf. "Still, we can check for airborne pollutants if you take this petri dish over to the office and leave it open on the attendance counter for twenty-four hours. Then we'll close it up and see what grows."

"All right!"

"Yeah!"

Darby guessed everyone else was imagining the creepy bacteria they'd be able to catch and grow, but she was picturing cracked pipes.

A slab of Sheetrock had sheered off the wall at

Cade's house near Crimson Vale. A refrigerator had tipped over. Either of those could crack underground pipes.

"Paradise has its price!" Mr. Silva raised his voice over the bell ringing to end class, and as Darby and Ann hustled out, they vowed, along with most of their classmates, not to drink from the school's fountains. Just in case.

By the time lunch break ended, there was definitely an epidemic of rumors. A guy claimed he'd overheard a custodian saying hundreds of contagious students had been sent home. Someone else said the illness was caused by foul water under the school.

Darby and Ann decided gossip had gotten way too crazy when they came into Algebra, their last class of the day, and heard Duckie, Darby's cousin, ask Coach Roffmore if it was true that the insulation in the classroom walls was mildewing with rat urine.

That was so ridiculous, Darby let her mind turn to the horses.

"Hoku, Navigator, Medusa, and Joker, and all the wild horses were swimming in that filthy water," she whispered to Ann.

"*Darby.*" Ann said her name pointedly, as if she'd missed something obvious.

"What?" she asked, glancing at Coach Roffmore.

"*You* were swimming in it." Ann frowned and looked toward the front of the room. "You and Duckie both."

Darby stared at her cousin Duxelles. Big, blond Duckie had always reminded her of a Viking. She looked strapping and strong, but bacteria wouldn't care. And Duckie had, in a rare act of kindness, rescued several wild colts from drowning.

Darby's mouth tasted sour as she recalled her fall from Hoku that same day. She'd taken in a gulp of that awful water that one of the firefighters had called junk soup.

Darby pulled up the neck of her pink polo shirt to cover her lips.

"Too late," Ann told her, and though she was smiling, her eyes looked worried.

Chapter Two

Darby's worries over water pollution floated away as soon as she rested her boot in the stirrup and swung into Navigator's saddle.

Cade had the rest of the day off. The young paniolo was not only Jonah's *hanai*'d son—in Hawaiian that meant fostered or adopted—he was also one of the hardest workers on the ranch and had been up at dawn, pounding fence posts into the ground.

Jonah had agreed Darby could ride with Cade into Crimson Vale to see if his mother, Dee, had returned to their tsunami-damaged house. Cade had tried to stay in touch with his mother, but his brutal stepfather, Manny Sharp, had made that difficult.

Now, though, Manny was in jail.

Jonah had told Darby to ride Navigator instead of Hoku. When she'd asked him why, he'd said, "All that wind and water left a few surprises in the valley. Count on that." Now, Darby was glad she'd taken her grandfather's advice.

The air had turned muggy. A fine mist fell and slicked over drying mud, but she didn't have to worry about her mount's footing or anything else. Smart and steady Navigator did it for her.

Cade rode Joker, his Appaloosa, down the slope into Crimson Vale, and Navigator followed.

Darby's body swayed in the saddle as she soaked up the music of the tropics. Rain tapped the dense foliage. Birds twittered, squawked, and sang *e-e-vee*. The distant roll and crash of waves drifted from the black sands of Night Digger Point Beach.

When she'd first seen Crimson Vale, Darby had thought this junglelike valley, with vines sprouting trumpet-shaped morning glory flowers all through the thickly packed trees, might be a magical place. Now that she'd lived a few months on Wild Horse Island, she was sure of it.

Violet shimmers danced in the rainbow that arched over a waterfall, dropping past black volcanic rock into a foaming pool of water.

Cade led her out of this enchantment toward the dismal home he'd shared with his mother and Manny. Cade had lived there until he was ten, when Jonah took him in after finding an injured Cade walking down the road leading Joker. Jonah had taken the boy to be patched up by Tutu, Darby's great-grandmother, and Cade had lived at 'Iolani Ranch ever since.

A quiver ran from Navigator's body through Darby's knees as a twilight-colored pony stepped into the path several yards ahead of them.

Cade turned in the saddle toward Darby, his face excited. Darby halted Navigator alongside him.

"Meet Honi, the pony," he said, rhyming the words.

The fairy-tale creature hurried forward to touch noses with Joker. Clearly, the two animals recognized each other.

"Your mother's pony?" Darby asked, and when the pony pointed its silvery ears toward her voice, Navigator began backing away.

She'd heard that some horses were afraid of ponies, but she never would have guessed it of Navigator.

Since she didn't want to tackle the steep trail behind them in reverse, Darby drove the big bay forward. He obeyed, then halted, but the Quarter Horse looked off into the trees instead of studying the pony.

"I should have realized that Manny was lying when he said Mom had stolen his truck and left the island. No way would she leave Honi behind."

Darby swallowed and tried to keep her face blank. Although she couldn't help admiring the strongly built pony with its high-set tail, fine-boned legs, and lively brown eyes, everything Cade had said about Dee indicated she cared more about her pony than her son.

"She's a beauty," Darby said.

"Half Arab and half Welsh," Cade said, and when the pony picked that moment to move closer to Navigator and lift her muzzle to neigh into his face, he added, "and all bossy."

Darby let Navigator sidestep away, but the pony followed, reminding her of her friend Heather's Siamese cat, which had always sought out the laps of people who preferred dogs.

"Does she run wild out here?" Darby asked.

She tried to revive her mental image of Cade's house, but she'd only been there once. What she did remember was Manny shooting at the wild horses, Kit threatening to teach Manny a lesson, and the dark, rising sea shadow of the tsunami.

"Mom lets her." Cade's tone was defensive. "She can find her way home."

"What does her name mean?" Darby asked, changing the subject.

"Kiss," Cade said, then hurried on. "Honi, go home. We'll follow you."

Much to Navigator's relief, the pony whirled on her back hooves and set off at a steady trot down the path.

Amazing, Darby thought. The pony really seemed to understand Cade and she obeyed him, even though he'd been away for years.

They followed Honi for about five minutes until she took off at a gallop, veering off the path and crashing through the foliage and down a slope thick with trees.

"I know where she's going." Cade sounded boyish, and Darby's spirits lifted along with his. "We'll take it a little slower," he assured her, and though Joker fretted and pulled at his bit, Cade kept him to a jog as they navigated the trail down the wet slope.

The big Quarter Horse descended cautiously, and when Cade and Joker disappeared into a dense tangle of trees, Navigator didn't hurry to catch up.

"I hope you know where you're going," Darby said.

In answer to her misgivings, the big bay detoured off the path, through a route so choked with vines he had to leap over them.

Once more the air turned moist, warm, and thick. Darby opened her mouth to get more oxygen. She hadn't thought about her asthma much lately, and had even caught herself going out and leaving her inhaler behind. That was another thing she would never have done back in smog-filled Los Angeles, but she rarely needed it these days.

She probably wouldn't need it now, either, but she'd just taken a deep, testing breath when Navigator carried her out of the trees.

"Ohh," Darby gasped.

The pond was an oasis, even in a world of emerald green. Honi had waded into the water-lily-strewn water and Cade had drawn rein to watch her.

"She's eating water lilies." He answered Darby's unspoken question when she rode up next to him. "She's always loved them."

Doesn't your mother feed her? Are they safe? Is Dee too lazy to care?

Darby held back the words. Obviously, Cade loved his mother despite her flaws. Insulting Dee would ruin their friendship.

Darby let her eyes wander until they halted on something brown and furry. She went still, trying not to scare off whatever it was until she realized it wasn't drinking at the water's edge. In fact, it didn't seem to move at all. The animal might not even be breathing.

"What's that?" Darby whispered. Even though she didn't point, Cade caught the direction of her eyes. "A ferret?" she guessed. "Or a weasel?"

"Dead mongoose," Cade said.

They brought their horses closer. Even though Darby felt sad at the unmoving little body, she looked closely.

It was about two feet long, and its brown fur had dried into dull clumps. With its head tucked under its stiff body, she couldn't see its face, and she was glad.

The horses paid no attention to it, which probably

meant, gross as it sounded even to her, that it didn't have much of a smell. She had the feeling it hadn't been there long.

"I've never seen a mongoose. But I remember *Rikki-Tikki-Tavi*." She'd didn't say it had been her mother who'd read her the story about a brave mongoose who'd saved the family that had adopted him as a pet.

"Do you think it drowned and just got washed up here?" Darby turned toward Cade. She hoped he agreed, before another, uglier possibility took shape in her mind.

"Must have."

Darby let out a breath. Cade would probably know. Besides, she'd seen too many creatures swept up by the tsunami, paddling to get free, not to know that was the most likely cause of the mongoose's death.

Even animals that survived the killer wave had been struck by debris or drowned in their exhausted struggle to reach land.

Darby didn't even know she'd been hyperventilating until her breaths slowed and Navigator shifted, feeling her relax.

"Or it could be somethin' in the water." Cade whistled shrilly. "Honi, get out of there!"

The pony lifted her head about a foot above the pond's surface but continued to chew on a water lily.

The water. Mud, malaria, the sick kids in the office . . .

"Honi!" Darby shouted with such force Navigator shied under her.

The silver-gray pony stood knee-deep in the water. She was soaking in it. She was eating a plant that had been immersed in it.

"Do you think the water poisoned the mongoose?" she asked, but Cade concentrated on unsnapping the leather strap that kept a rope coiled on his saddle. Shaking it out caught the pony's attention.

With a disgruntled snort, Honi's head jerked up. She tossed her forelock away from her eyes and glared at Cade.

"Can you rope her?" Darby asked.

Cade ignored her, rolling his wrist before raising the rope and spinning it into a loop above his head.

How did he do that? Darby wondered, but Honi wasn't at all curious. She knew what came next and she didn't want to be dragged out of the pond.

With a long, splashing lunge, Honi reached the shore. She shook herself before breaking into a run, but even then she didn't release the water-lily stem trailing from her mouth.

"Come on." Cade sounded grim, as if his fears were the same as Darby's, but they didn't talk about the possibility of tainted water as they headed toward the tan house standing at a slant on the hillside ahead.

Honi dashed through the gully holding the taro field, but Darby and Cade rode around. Though the earthen walls protecting the plants had collapsed and once-green leaves were pasted flat by dried mud, it still didn't seem right to trample the only evidence that real farming had taken place here.

Darby looked up at the house Cade had once lived in and thought that the sheets of stucco that had shaken off the house during earthquakes had given it the patchy appearance of a giraffe.

Just as Cade had predicted, Honi had come all the way home. She stood sniffing the wooden porch. Amid its broken boards, she found something to lip up and eat.

As Darby rode nearer, she saw a few oat flakes.

"Mom's been here to feed Honi," Cade said, noticing the same thing.

Darby didn't contradict him, even though she knew volunteers from the Animal Rescue Society had patrolled areas hard-hit by the tsunami looking for needy animals.

"She's either asleep or gone." Cade's voice sounded tight. "Let's put Joker and Navigator in back before we check inside."

A slick, steep hillside rose behind the house. Before they came to it there was a small corral with a trough that held a few inches of rainwater.

"I should stay with the horses," Darby said. She really didn't want to go inside Manny's lair.

"Suit yourself," Cade said, but in the instant before he turned to go back to the front door, Darby saw disappointment in his brown eyes.

Nice friend you are, Darby told herself. *How bad can it be?*

"They'll probably be fine," Darby said to the empty clearing and hurried after Cade.

As she came around the corner of the tilted house, Cade pushed open the unlocked door. "Mom?" he shouted. "Are you here? It's me, Cade."

No one answered.

Darby entered the silent house behind Cade.

Almost silent, she thought as water dripped through a cracked glass pane, over the windowsill, and onto the floor.

The refrigerator that had tipped over two weeks ago still lay there, but someone had brought in black plastic bags and they'd been piled, lumpy and full, against one wall.

"She's been back since we were here." Cade considered an ashtray overflowing with stubbed-out cigarettes. His teeth clamped together. The skin pulled taut across the bump on his jawbone.

He banged on the bedroom door. "Mom!" When there was no reply, he opened it a little and peered in. "She's not here," he reported. He disappeared inside and came back a moment later. "Her stuff's still here. I told you she wouldn't leave Honi."

"That's good," Darby said, but inside, she wasn't so sure.

Wouldn't it be better if Dee got out of Cade's life once and for all? He loved working as a paniolo. He was content as Jonah's son and valued as a member of the ranch family.

Of course, she was leaving out the part about loving his mother. Darby sighed, glad Cade was more interested in detective work than in her reaction to this place.

"I don't see Manny's truck," Cade observed as he looked through the slats of grimy blinds. "Maybe she took it into town. Mind if we wait here just a little while?"

"No problem." Darby pushed some junk mail to the end of the couch, revealing fabric pocked with small, round cigarette burns.

Cade perched on the couch's arm, and all at once Darby saw what she'd been missing.

Cade was only acting like nothing was out of the ordinary, like this was the normal state of things. In fact, Cade was barely controlling his disgust.

Both fists were clenched as he said, "I can still smell Manny in this place."

"He's in jail—"

"For now," Cade snapped.

"Trafficking in antiquities is a pretty serious charge, isn't it?" Darby asked. "And politically, you know"— Darby searched for the right word—"sensitive?"

"I guess," Cade admitted.

"Think about it," Darby insisted. "Hawaiians care about their culture. Most can't stand the idea of one of their own selling off their history, their heritage.

Any judge with good sense will put him away forever and—"

Until Cade gently pushed away her index finger, she didn't realize she'd been shaking it at him for emphasis.

"Sorry," she said, then tidied her ponytail as if it mattered.

Maybe it was all wishful thinking, but maybe she was right. She was feeling pretty optimistic, until Cade muttered something she couldn't understand.

"What?"

"I said, what if she takes him back?" Cade asked.

"Why would she? Are you kidding?"

"Why did they get together in the first place? I mean, I know what she says, but lots of single mothers do okay." Cade stopped, as if he felt disloyal, then stood up and paced around the room.

Cade's right. Dee could have found child care and a job. Lots of single mothers do that, Darby thought. *My mom did. Dee didn't have to live with a criminal who beat her son.* It was getting harder to keep her opinion to herself, but Cade was upset enough without her piling on his mother.

"I can't just abandon her, you know. Even though Manny was a creep, he fed her and stuff."

"I know," Darby said.

"But I can't let her keep on this way, either."

Darby barely heard him, because she'd thought of something worse. What if there really was a plague?

Dee could be out in the forest, alone and sick. But Darby didn't need to add to Cade's scary thoughts.

A heavy silence fell between them.

They must have waited an hour when Cade finally gave up.

"I wish her cell phone worked. If she hasn't paid the bill it means she's broke," Cade grumbled.

He found a pen and stood ready to write a note on the back of an envelope, but then he looked at Darby. "What should we do with Honi? There's rain-water in the trough"—he nodded toward the corral behind the house—"but is it enough? And if I leave her loose, she'll go back to the pond and, well, that mongoose . . ."

"Uh-huh," Darby said. "That worries me, too."

Cade tapped the pen on the paper. He looked so confused, Darby tried to help him decide what to do next.

"You've got a rope. Catch Honi and bring her home with us. Write your mom a note letting her know Honi is with you," she said, pointing at the paper. "So she won't worry."

"Yes, ma'am," Cade said, in a pretty good imitation of a western drawl.

With a smile, Cade wrote quickly and lightly until he jabbed the pen point down in what looked like a final period. He picked up the paper and reread the note.

He was clearing a space on the kitchen counter,

when something big—probably Navigator—bumped the back of the house.

Then, before Darby could make sense of Cade's change in expression, he wadded the note into a ball and threw it against the wall.

 Chapter Three

"What's wrong?" Darby asked.

"I can't bring Honi back to the ranch. What if she's already sick? And contagious?"

Cade decided the best he could do for the pony was hook open the corral gate, so that she could drink from the trough. He put out the last of the hay, then said, "I've got to find my mom. I hate to ask Jonah for time off, but I don't know what else to do."

Darby didn't, either, not right then, but she'd think hard on the ride back to the ranch. Maybe she'd come up with something.

They rode away from the tilted house. Honi walked as far as the edge of the ruined taro patch, but then she stopped. She stayed behind, waiting for Dee.

* * *

Darby made it home in time to help Megan put together a big shrimp salad. That was a good thing, because the two of them were in charge of dinner that night.

"I'm glad you remembered," Megan said as Darby burst through Sun House's front door and shucked off her boots.

"Of course I did," Darby said, but they almost hadn't made it in time, because Cade, at her urging, had stopped to bury the dead mongoose.

"Wow, give us a bath, why don't you!"

"Sorry," Darby said. She hadn't meant to turn on the water full blast.

Megan watched as Darby began scrubbing from fingertips to elbows, trying to wash off all remnants of the sad house in Crimson Vale.

"Was it pretty gross out at Cade's place?" Megan whispered. "Never mind, you don't have to tell me."

Ten minutes later, they were serving dinner on the lanai, just as they'd promised Aunty Cathy they would. And Jonah actually rubbed his hands together in anticipation at the smell of the garlic bread they served with the salad.

Darby's gloom had lifted and both girls were feeling pretty proud of themselves by the time the evening news came on the living room TV with an announcement that made them even happier.

All schools would be closed until the Health Department could make inspections to determine the cause of an outbreak of flulike symptoms among students.

Darby wasn't surprised, and she wasn't feeling sick, but she didn't stop worrying about the horses until Megan bounced up, grabbed Darby's wrists, and dragged her to her feet, then began dancing in delight.

She couldn't resist Megan's gladness, even when Jonah shouted, "Hey! That just means I've got me two more workers for tomorrow!"

"Killjoy," Megan called after Jonah as he left the living room for the lanai.

"For sure," Jonah said, but once he was outside, Darby watched her grandfather look skyward. Then he turned west, as though he could foretell the weather by the breeze on his face.

Jonah was known as a horse charmer, and there were some—including her, at times—who thought he'd passed his intuition for horse communication on to Darby.

But he had more than a knack with horses, Darby thought. Jonah's sensitivity to the world around him was so precise, sometimes it was spooky.

"That's a wet wind," he said, just loud enough to be heard.

Darby realized that she'd rarely thought about the weather before coming to Moku Lio Hihiu. Of course they *had* weather back in Pacific Pinnacles, where she'd lived before coming here. But it was usually just sunny weather, filtered through layers of smoke and fog. Unless there was an actual smog alert, since bad air triggered her asthma, weather wasn't as important.

"You didn't listen to the rest of the news story, did you?" Aunty Cathy's low voice distracted Darby. She and Megan dropped hands. "The ARC is coming around checking wells for contamination. Until then, they want ranchers and farmers to reduce water use by ten percent."

"The ark?" Darby asked. "Like Noah?"

Megan laughed and shook her head. "No, it's A—R—C." She paused between each letter. "It's the Agricultural—what is it, Mom?"

"Agricultural Resource Conservation division," Aunty Cathy supplied.

Before she explained the agency, Jonah strode back into the house, muttering, "State bureaucrats, but they've been all over the island in their slickers and hip boots, inspecting flumes, pipes, and reservoirs ever since the first earthquake. Gotta give 'em credit for that."

"So, you'll go along with the cutback?" Megan asked.

"What do you think, I'm an outlaw?" Jonah looked annoyed rather than insulted. "Besides, there's no reason not to go along. There's another storm coming, I've got two sturdy girls to roll out rain barrels," he said, counting on his fingers, "and they can pour the caught water into the tack-room trough, Hoku's trough, and the dogs' dishes."

Darby was pretty sure that didn't amount to ten percent, but she didn't say so.

"Sure, I'll go along. But I know my well. When the ARC checks, it'll be sweet and pure as the year my father and grandfather dug it."

"Girls, you ought to go get those barrels out now," Aunty Cathy said.

"I thought it wasn't supposed to rain until morning," Megan said, stretching lazily.

"If you have so much faith in the weatherman that you won't mind getting out of bed and running out there in your nightie to roll out the barrels if he's wrong . . ." Aunty Cathy let her voice trail off.

"Mom," Megan moaned. "That's not funny."

Darby and Megan went outside and right away Darby felt the Kona winds. As soon as she realized the breeze carried no ash to make her wheeze, Darby squared her shoulders and remembered what Jonah had just said. He had two sturdy girls to help him.

Her? Sturdy? Darby's friend Heather, back in Pacific Pinnacles, would laugh at that.

So many things had changed since she came to live in Hawaii. She'd arrived skinny, with a droopy black ponytail, and often sick with asthma. Though she loved horses with all her heart, she'd never ridden one, and she'd shown up at the ranch with an armful of books and her pockets stuffed with pills and inhalers.

Now she rarely needed her inhaler, and she felt stronger. She spent every minute she wasn't at school working with animals, exploring the island on horseback, or caring for Hoku, her mustang filly.

Both girls had paused to inspect the sky for rain clouds, so they'd only gone a few steps when two of the five ranch dogs trotted over to meet them. Peach licked their hands while Bart bounded around them.

The rising wind ruffled the dogs' fur, and even when they were petted, the dogs' ears stayed upright and alert. They knew a storm was coming.

"Meg?" Aunty Cathy called from the kitchen window, but her face was hidden by flapping curtains. "If you see Cade, tell him I've got to go into town tomorrow for my final doctor's appointment and I'll check for word about Dee."

"Okay," Megan called back, but a boom of thunder, followed by thudding hooves, stopped her from saying more.

Darby and Megan exchanged wide-eyed glances.

"The cremellos," Darby said. "There's no water trough in the round pen, is there?"

"No. Horses almost never stay loose in there. Usually, it's just for training."

They watched the pale horses move together like a flight of gulls in the round pen.

The cremello horses had been a gift with strings from Darby's great-aunt, Babe Borden. She owned Sugar Sands Cove, a luxury resort, and had worked out an arrangement with Jonah to allow her guests to come ride at 'Iolani Ranch. But the cremellos' five-acre pasture, which would include a picturesque hill just to the right of the gravel driveway, was still being fenced by Kit, Kimo, and Cade.

Eventually, the pasture would have a trough of its own, but now the horses had to be led to water.

"Is that why he said we had to fill the trough by the tack shed?" Darby asked.

Leading each of the cremellos to water several times a day was a small chore when the trough had an automatic flow valve that kept it full. But if the trough had to be filled by bucket, the job would be a big one.

"Horses drink five to twelve gallons each day," Darby said. "Multiply that by six cremellos, plus any horses that have a drink after they've been out working, and that's—"

"—a whole lotta haulin'," Megan complained. "Jonah should pretend that we're not here. If school wasn't closed that's where we'd be: *not here*."

Darby laughed. "I don't think Jonah pretends much."

"I'd say not even when he was a little kid, if it weren't for that wooden horse in his library," Megan agreed.

A raindrop plopped on Darby's nose. "Here it comes," she said.

"And the barrels are under cover down by the pigpen, and we haven't even started," Megan said. "I guess we should grab a couple slickers out of the tack room."

"It's too hot," Darby said, "and it'll scare Hoku."

"Do what you want, but I'm going to be modeling banana yellow for the next half hour," Megan said.

While Megan searched for a slicker, Darby ran on ahead and stopped next to Hoku's corral fence. Since that first raindrop, the sky seemed to be holding its breath. Tension charged every molecule of air, as if they were just waiting for lightning to set loose the rain.

Hoku trotted back and forth, agitated by the weather. At least Darby thought that was what was wrong. Hoku had eaten every wisp of her dinnertime hay, but even in the dim light, her sorrel coat glistened with sweat as her brown eyes watched her human.

Darby loved Hoku completely. They had bonded when the wild filly had been hit by a bus back on War Drum Flats in Nevada. She'd lain beside the injured horse in the snow for a long time until help finally arrived. During that vigil, Darby had talked to the horse and sung to her, and somehow attachments had grown between them, mind to mind, heart to heart.

But Hoku was still wild, and Darby was still new to the world of horses. They were learning together.

"I know you lived through thunderstorms in Nevada," Darby scolded softly. "And you didn't have any soft-hearted humans to talk you out of worrying."

But she'd had her herd, Darby thought. Mustangs learned when they were shaky-legged foals that safety is always with the herd.

"I'm a pretty sad substitute for a herd, is that what you're thinking?"

The filly's lips and nostrils quivered with a silent neigh as she looked over Darby's head. Hoku knew 'Iolani's saddle horses and broodmares weren't far away, and no matter how much she loved Darby, Hoku longed to run with others of her kind.

The filly shied, rolling her eyes white as Megan came rustling up to Darby in her bright yellow slicker.

"Should I do anything?" Darby asked Megan. "She's scared in there alone but it's not a big-enough emergency—not like the earthquake—to let her out to be with the others."

Jonah had told Darby that isolating Hoku much of the time would help cement the bond between girl and horse. So far, he was right.

Suddenly, Hoku rocked onto her hind legs, then brought both front hooves down together.

"What does that mean?" Darby asked.

"It's—" Megan frowned in concentration as the filly repeated the movement. "I have no idea. Does it look to you like she's smashing something?"

"Yeah, but there's nothing there," Darby said.

"And you're not picking up any horse charmer vibes?"

"None," Darby said flatly.

They watched the horse until Megan shrugged. "You're going to get wet anyway. Go in and be her buddy. Here, I got a carrot from the tack room for Pigolo, but it might distract Hoku. I'll wait for you, but we should get going with those barrels."

Darby took the carrot intended for the rescued piglet and stuck it in her pocket. She unlatched the corral gate, slipped inside, and fixed the gate closed behind her.

"What's this?" Darby murmured to her horse.

Rather than calming Hoku, Darby's approach made the mustang even more nervous. She circled the corral at a strange gait. Darby had never watched five-gaited horses like American saddlebreds in action, but such energy went into every one of Hoku's high-stepping moves, she thought this looked something like that gait called a rack.

The splash of white on the filly's chest—the mark that had earned her the name Hoku, "star" in Hawaiian—came right at Darby each time Hoku passed.

Darby tightened her ponytail and finally the filly slid to a stop. The gesture was a secret between them.

"Hey, baby, don't be afraid. I'm here."

Hoku's pinned-back ears flicked forward at the sound of Darby's voice.

"It's okay." Darby forgot Megan, the weather, everything but this little patch of earth and the calm she hoped Hoku could draw from her.

"Good girl." She moved close enough to stroke Hoku's side. "You're such a good girl."

Thunder clapped once again and Hoku shied, bumping Darby almost off her feet. But Darby didn't move away. She kept talking.

"It's a little thunder, no big deal."

The filly paced along the fence and Darby stayed with her, humming a medieval-sounding song her mother liked. She didn't know why it popped into her mind. It could be because it mentioned parsley, sage, rosemary, and thyme. If she could drift the rangeland smell of sage to her filly's nostrils, she would have, but even the melody made the filly stop with a lowered head.

Still humming, Darby listened as the filly's breathing slowed. Darby rested her forehead on Hoku's neck. Could she really feel the mustang's coursing blood begin to slow? Were they both hypnotized by the melody?

Hoku sniffed the feathery top of the carrot in Darby's pocket, then nudged it.

Darby broke off a piece and let the filly eat. Then Darby walked and Hoku followed. Smiling, Darby stopped and gave Hoku a second piece of carrot. They moved together until they reached the gate.

"One more." Darby balanced the last piece of carrot on her flattened palm.

Hoku drooled carrot juice on Darby's arm, took the final offering, and chewed calmly, watching as

Darby slipped outside the corral to rejoin Megan.

"Nice work," she praised Darby, giving her a little shove to urge her into a jog. "You really settled her down."

Darby glanced back over her shoulder. "Will she worry if I'm out of sight and there's more thunder?"

"I'm not sure," Megan admitted. "But I doubt you'll have such an easy time settling *Jonah* down, if we don't get to work."

The next clap of thunder came when Darby was halfway to the pigpen. She heard Hoku bolt around her corral and called back, "It's okay, girl. No big deal."

She tried to keep her voice reassuring despite Megan's impatience. Without speaking, Megan made a quick jerk of her chin, hinting they should keep creeping away, and they did.

Darby recalled seeing her dad's new wife, Angel, slowly easing out of the room when one of her fussy babies was finally starting to fall asleep. Something in this silent departure reminded her of that.

The rainstorm arrived just as Megan and Darby rolled the last of the large barrels into position near the tack room and stood it up.

Since they hadn't asked for details on how they'd get the water from the barrels to the troughs, they set them near the dog kennel, Hoku's corral, and the tack room, figuring they could siphon the water into the troughs.

"This ought to do it," Megan shouted to be heard over the drumming rain.

The downpour took only seconds to soak Darby's hair. Streams coursed down her ponytail and into the neck of her shirt while rain dripped daintily off Megan's yellow hood.

Darby's jeans clung like a coarse second skin, making her step stiff-legged as she and Megan walked past the bunkhouse.

Kit and Cade must have been inside, because lamplight and the sound of Kit strumming a guitar floated into the night, making the bunkhouse feel warm and cozy.

Darby was shivering, hoping she could commandeer Sun House's only bathroom for a warm, deep bath, when she heard Sass barking in the lower pasture.

The bunkhouse door opened. A rectangle of light turned the raindrops gold and made Darby and Megan squint up at Cade.

"Sounds like Sass has something cornered," he said.

"Can you *hear* in the dark, too?" Megan teased Cade, since he was known for his ability to see in almost nonexistent light.

"When it goes on without letup like that, who couldn't?" Cade asked.

He'd already pulled on his dark green poncho and tugged his hala hat down to cover his hair by the time

Darby realized he planned to go see what had the dog so excited.

He stepped outside into the darkness and rain, then whistled.

 Chapter Four

"You're not really going down there, are you?" Megan asked.

Cade's smile said he planned to do just that.

"Kit 'n' me drew lots and I lost," Cade said, "but I'm hopin' Sass comes to me with the rest of the dogs, so I *don't* have to go down there."

"I know Sass is good with horses," Megan said, "but he'll also hunt anything that lives in a burrow."

Whatever Sass was after didn't fascinate the other dogs. His barking went on in the lower pasture, as three other Australian shepherds—Peach, Jack, and Jill—came skittering through the mud, swirling around Cade's legs in answer to his whistle.

"Oh!" Megan blurted, remembering her mother's

message. "Mom said to tell you she'll check for news of Dee when she goes into town tomorrow." Megan pulled the sides of the yellow hood away from her eyes as though she wanted a better view of how her words affected Cade.

But Cade didn't look at Megan and his expression was blank when he glanced at Darby. She gave her head a faint shake, assuring him she hadn't been gossiping about him, his mother, or the state of their house, before Cade had had a chance to talk to Jonah.

Megan shifted, waiting for Cade to respond.

Say something, Darby silently willed him. But Cade didn't.

"Hey," Megan began.

"Did you hear that?" Cade asked.

"Did you hear *me*?" Megan insisted.

Just then Bart pulled himself up the grassy hillside and into the light. Panting, he rolled on the ground in front of Cade.

"I'm not scratching that muddy belly," Cade said.

Megan turned toward Darby with an expression that said she thought both Cade and Bart were adorable, but she didn't want them to know it.

Darby liked Cade fine. He'd proven he'd be there for her if things got tough, and she tried to be there for him, since she considered him half brother and half friend.

But Megan liked Cade in a different way. They weren't quite boyfriend and girlfriend, but Darby figured they were headed in that direction.

"I heard," Cade said finally. "Please tell your mom thanks." Cade looked away from them both, toward the incessant barking. "I'll give him a few more minutes."

"And then—"

Cade's second whistle interrupted Megan's sentence, but she kept on, hands on hips.

"—what? You're not going to go down there—"

"I'll lock up the rest of 'em first."

Cade walked toward the kennel with the dogs trailing him.

Muttering and shaking her head, Megan strode toward Sun House.

Falling into step beside her, Darby said, "I guess that's his job."

The rain and wind had slacked off and the night felt warm, but Megan made a wide gesture that took in the darkness and said, "It's not even safe."

The words were barely out of her mouth before they heard a whine, and Sass came trotting down the dirt road toward them.

"You sure took your time," Megan reproached the dog.

"Are we glad to see you," Darby greeted him.

Sass stopped a few feet away. Head high, tail straight up like an exclamation point, he barked directly at them.

"We're not going down there to crawl into muddy

holes with you," Darby said.

Shivering despite his persistent barking, the wet dog needed care. It only took Megan one glance to know what to do.

"Keep him here. I'll go get a towel." Megan darted away.

Darby tried to do as she'd been told, but Sass wouldn't come close enough for her to touch him, let alone get a grip on his collar or ruff.

He trotted back down the road, whining. He wanted her to follow him. When she wouldn't, he grew frustrated, and his barks turned into high-pitched yapping.

"Here to me," Megan ordered as she came back out of the house with a towel.

Sass stood in the beam from the front porch light, hesitating. He was not allowed to disobey a direct command, but he bounced in mock playfulness, trying once more to get someone to follow him.

"Sass." Megan lowered her voice in a pretty good imitation of Jonah's. "Here. To. Me."

Eyes reproachful and tongue lolling, he went to Megan. He let himself be toweled off, but whined the entire time. Once he was dry, Megan inspected the dog from paw pads to the tips of his blue merle ears.

"You're not hurt," she informed him.

At the clang of the kennel gate, Sass pounced down the road a few feet and made a last plea with a yodeling sound.

"The thing is, we don't want to go hunt squirmy things," Megan said. Her slicker crinkled as she crossed her arms.

With a huff of surrender, Sass wagged his lowered tail and trotted off toward Cade and the other dogs.

It was morning before Darby gave Sass another thought.

Jonah's voice invaded her dreams. "You go on down with Cade. See about that colt."

Darby sat up in bed and used both hands to push curtains of black hair away from her face.

"What?" she asked.

"You heard me."

Boots clomped down the hall, the front door closed, and her grandfather was gone.

Darby stared at her bedside clock. Six thirty. Okay. She hadn't expected to sleep late even if school was canceled. The pasture fence had to be finished for the cremellos. The Agricultural Department of What-ever people would probably show up to enforce the new regulation. . . .

All at once Jonah's words soaked into her brain.

. . . go on down with Cade. See about that colt. . . .

Darby's feet hit the floor. For a bleary minute, she wondered why there were no ready-to-wear jeans on her bedroom floor. But they were wet, of course, tossed into the laundry room. She opened a drawer, grabbed fresh jeans, a bright green T-shirt, and socks.

As she walked toward the front door, it dawned on Darby that Sass hadn't been after vermin last night. He'd been trying to tell them something was wrong down in the broodmare pasture.

Judging from what Jonah had just said, at least Cade had listened.

Once she'd pulled on her socks and boots, Darby bolted out of Sun House. She was looking down, concentrating on winding an elastic around her hair as she walked, and nearly collided with Jonah.

He was leading Navigator. The big brown Quarter Horse was trying to outpace his master, heading toward Darby as if he hadn't seen her in months, even though they'd gone on a long ride just yesterday.

Jonah didn't think the gelding's eagerness was at all cute, and he let the horse know by making a shh-ing sound. Navigator fell into place behind him. Just the same, Jonah stopped and made Navigator back up a few steps before he allowed him to go forward.

Discipline was an every-hour-of-every-day thing on this ranch, but the reprimand didn't keep Navigator from watching Darby approach and it didn't stop Darby from appreciating the horse all over again.

Navigator had selected Darby as his person on the day she'd arrived at 'Iolani Ranch.

He was the first horse she'd ridden in her entire life. That would have earned him a place in her heart, Darby thought, even if he hadn't been the perfect beginner mount for her.

"Shouldn't I do my chores first?" she asked when her grandfather and Navigator reached her.

"I'll get them started. You need to see what a colicky horse looks like."

As she took the reins, her grandfather's promise that she'd take over the ranch one day replayed in her mind. Recognizing what was wrong with a sick colt was a single fact among the millions she'd have to learn if that dream could really come true.

And, though she wanted to know which colt, and what colic was, she didn't ask. Another fact she'd already learned was her grandfather's probable response to those questions. Jonah would cross his arms and ask why she didn't just go see for herself.

"Don't look so scared," Jonah said. "I'll send Kit out when he comes back from checking the cattle in Upper Sugar Mill, or if Kimo ever shows up, I'll come myself."

Kimo was often late, but she was surprised he'd fail to show up when there was so much to do. Still, Darby didn't comment on Kimo's shortcomings. She just lifted one shoulder in a shrug, like the guys did.

Next, she led Navigator to a side hill so that she could reach his left stirrup without hopping around trying to stab her boot toe through it with Jonah watching. Luck was with her on her first try; she swung into the saddle with ease.

Smiling, she reined Navigator back toward Jonah and asked, "How long's Cade been down there?"

"Since about three," Jonah said. "Sass dug out of the kennel. Surprised you didn't hear the others tellin' on him."

"Me, too," Darby began.

"So, you waiting for an invitation to ride down there?" Jonah asked.

"No," she said. "See ya later."

Darby's mind spun as she put Navigator into a trot.

Colic. She'd heard the term before, but she was pretty sure it had been used about babies. Colic affected the stomach, didn't it? And hadn't she read that horses were physically incapable of throwing up?

She reined Navigator to the right and set him on the trail that zigzagged down the hillside to the pastures below.

Darby picked out the pink-roan coat of Megan's horse, Tango. She saw the elegant dappled gray named Lady Wong and, patrolling the pasture called Borderland, she spotted Kanaka Luna. The bay stallion pranced and tossed his rippling black mane, showing off for Navigator and Darby, informing them he was king of all he surveyed.

But Darby barely noticed Luna's display. She was wondering if colts died from colic.

The day was so bright, Darby squinted against the sun, then ducked a little, trying to avoid the breeze carrying dew drops from the tree leaves.

The broodmares stood with their tails to the rain

and their foals tucked against their sides. Some of the babies whinnied fretfully. It was June. Summer was on its way. Their growing muscles told them to romp and race, but a stronger message kept them near the grown horses.

The mares swished their tails. They strayed no more than a body length from one another, and they stood in the shade instead of the warm sunlight, staying near Blue Ginger and her foal, forming a wall between those two and Joker, who was ground-tied nearby.

At least that's what it looked like to Darby. Which was weird, because the mares knew Cade's Appaloosa gelding.

They must have sensed something was wrong.

Cade wasn't astride his black-splattered gray horse. Instead he stood with Blue Ginger's foal. Cade had made a sling of his arms to hold—Blue Moon, that was his name!—up on his feet.

Cade looked worn-out. Once his eyes found Darby, he was too weary to move his gaze elsewhere.

"You've been at this a while," Darby called to him.

He nodded. Darby lifted her reins and clucked at Navigator. The gelding lengthened his stride, taking her toward Cade, the blue roan, and her foal.

Despite Cade's grip, the little horse's head was down and moving back and forth in a strange way. One tiny front hoof pawed the ground and patches of sweat marked his light brown coat.

Darby dismounted, left Navigator ground-tied near Joker, and walked slowly up to Cade.

"Can I have a turn?" she asked.

Cade started to refuse, but weariness won out, because he nodded and Darby's disappointment turned to trepidation.

"Just tell me how," Darby said.

"Put your arms in front of or behind mine. Then, when I take my arms away, move 'em where mine were."

Darby did, but when Cade's arms relinquished the foal to her, she gave a grunt of surprise.

"Heavier than he looks, yeah?" Cade asked.

"Yeah," Darby said, but she didn't care. She was overcome with tenderness for the little heart beating against her wrists.

The foal's head whipped around and at first she thought he might rake her with his bared teeth, but he just rubbed his face against her arm.

This close, Darby could see white hair sprinkled through Blue Moon's fawn-colored coat. She wondered if he'd be roan or buckskin or bay like his father, when he grew up. She hoped she had the opportunity to find out.

"Poor baby," Darby crooned to the foal.

"He's doing better," Cade said. "We just need to keep him moving."

"Do *you* think it's colic?" Darby asked.

"I'm not so—hey, great. Here comes Kit."

The buckaroo rode in from the direction of the cattle herds, black Stetson pulled low over his eyes. He rode a half-trained grulla named Conch, and the broodmares were anything but happy to see the gelding's excitement.

"No ground-tying for you," Kit said. He balanced in his left stirrup, accustoming the gelding to the fact that he was dismounting before climbing down.

The considerate and experienced move made Darby feel better already, though her arms trembled from the foal's weight.

The mares fretted as Kit led Conch closer, but they trusted the cowboy and allowed him and the gelding through.

People often mistook Kit for a native Hawaiian because of his straight black hair, but he was really half Shoshone, a Native American from Nevada. He was a former rodeo rider who had smashed up one wrist in a rodeo fall. It was enough to end his rodeo career, although he was still amazing with horses. One of his rodeo pals, a guy named Pani, had helped Kit get the foreman's job at the ranch.

Darby couldn't have explained why she thought Kit was worried. He wasn't frowning and he didn't really look ill at ease, but she could tell something was wrong.

"Haven't seen Kimo, I s'pose," he said as he squatted to look the foal over without touching him.

"No," Darby and Cade said together.

Kit kept one rein in his hand. His other hand touched the turquoise rock on his leather string necklace.

"You think it's colic?" he asked Cade, just as Darby had minutes ago.

Cade shrugged.

"A lot of bacteria's gotten into the main reservoir near Hapuna. We should be fine, but ARC's got an agriculture and health department team comin' to check out the well. If they see him like this, they could shut us down. Cricket's goin' to come with them if she can get away from the store."

Cricket Pukai was an Animal Rescue Society volunteer and Kit's girlfriend. Darby admired everything about her, but what did she have to do with the water situation? Was Kit implying she could help them face down the ARC team?

"Eyes're a little glassy," Kit observed as he turned toward her. "How's his belly feel?"

How would I know? Darby wondered, but when Cade answered, "Tight, but not puffed up," she understood Kit's question.

She concentrated on the feel of the foal's body against her arms.

"Not drum-skin tight," she said, "more like he's had a little too much to eat."

Kit's gaze shifted between Darby and Cade.

"Hard to know what to hope for," he said. "Bacteria could hurt 'em all, but colic kills 'em when pressure from gas causes heart failure."

"Not always!" Darby exclaimed, but she heard the question in her voice.

"Not even usually," Kit assured her. "He's not over-fed. I can't figure him getting spoiled grain anywhere." Looking thoughtful, as though he'd gone down a mental list of what caused the condition, he considered the wide, green pastures. "Any poisonous weeds I haven't come across yet?"

Cade shook his head.

"He been rolling or biting at his flanks?"

"No."

By now the foal had grown so heavy in Darby's arms, she wasn't surprised to see his long eyelashes were closed.

Noticing her baby was asleep, Blue Ginger stepped closer. She took breaths so deep, they lifted strands of Darby's hair.

"What are we going to do with him?" Darby whispered.

Jonah didn't approve of pampering the horses. He refused to treat them like pets. To him, the Quarter Horses, dogs, and other animals on the place were working partners.

Darby had never seen a vet visit 'Iolani Ranch, but they probably didn't need one. The combined knowledge of Jonah, Aunty Cathy, Kit, and Kimo must have amounted to a couple of degrees in veterinary medicine.

Still, Blue Moon was so little. . . .

"We'll take him up where we can keep an eye on him." Kit lifted his head toward Sun House. "Can't spend all day checking on him. Too much work to be done."

Cade drew in a breath that only Darby noticed. Cade wanted to go look for his mom in town, but how could he leave the ranch with the ARC people on their way, the cremellos' pasture fence still to be finished, and Blue Moon's health shaky?

Darby hoped Aunty Cathy had picked up Dee's trail in town.

"Will he walk?" Kit asked.

"Don't know," Cade said. "We can try."

"Wake up, baby," Darby said as she slowly removed her arms.

Blue Moon's eyelids flapped open, his tail spun in a corkscrew move, and he jumped a few steps toward his mother before he stopped, yawned, and lay down.

Cade knelt beside the foal and tried to push him up, but Blue Moon just flopped flat.

It wasn't until Kit opened the foal's mouth to check the color of his gums that Blue Moon's spirit returned. He did *not* like the cowboy's probing fingers. Pawing the grass with his front hooves, he got halfway up.

Blue Ginger rammed into Darby's shoulder, pushing past the half circle of humans to her foal. Did Kit and Cade sense the anxiety streaming off the mare, like she could? Darby tried to stroke the horse's blue-gray neck, but Blue Ginger jerked away.

The mare knew the foal had to get back on his feet, but she was trying to let him do it on his own.

"He'll be okay," Darby told the mare, but Kit picked that moment to insist the foal get back on his hooves.

"Move Mom off a ways," he told Darby.

Blue Ginger wore no halter or bridle, so Darby grabbed a handful of mane, clucked, and started walking.

The mare's body shifted toward Darby, but her hooves stayed still.

"Mount up," Kit said. "Ride toward home on Navigator."

Darby did as Kit asked, but of course Blue Ginger didn't follow. Why had Kit thought she would abandon her sick baby?

Darby looked over her shoulder to see Cade was once again shoving lightly against the foal's hindquarters. Nothing. Then Kit moved in to swat the foal more forcefully on his rump.

Darby winced. It was unlike Kit to be rough with any animal, but she understood as she heard him talking to the foal.

"Move, little boy," he commanded. "Walk it off now, or you might not get another chance."

 Chapter Five

In a flurry of hooves, Blue Moon lurched up, then moved slowly and steadily behind his mother. Cade was back on Joker, raising one hand, hazing the mare after Darby.

They'd reached the ridge and turned up the driveway toward Sun House when Darby noticed two things: Kimo's truck still wasn't here, but a light blue vehicle with writing on the door was.

The ARC team, she remembered. Agricultural Resource Conservation? She was pretty sure that was it.

Navigator's gait slowed as two men, deep in conversation with Jonah, looked up at her. Darby's old shyness made her stare down at her saddle horn.

The hooves behind her changed tempo, and Darby knew the mare and foal had picked up her anxiety.

Shake it off, Darby told herself as Kit and Cade kept the two horses moving after her. *You're not the big attraction. They're here to check out the well.*

She lifted her chin and straightened her spine, trying to ride with the natural grace she'd observed in every other Kealoha on horseback.

"What now?" Jonah shouted as if fate was picking on him.

"Colic." Kit confirmed Jonah's diagnosis with an almost indifferent tone. "Only brought 'em up because we're too busy to fuss over him down there."

Darby's first impression of the two men was that they were muddy and grateful for the coffee Jonah had just given them. Although the sun dominated the cloudy sky, the men cupped their hands around their mugs as if they needed the warmth. They'd probably been wet for a while.

When she glanced up to take a good look at them, she decided the two men were physical opposites. She was trying to place the slim one with slicked-down black hair. Though they hadn't been introduced, she recognized the name badge on his uniform and his presence made her smile as she realized where she'd seen him before.

Mr. Nomi looked slight-bodied, but she'd seen him in action and he was tougher than he looked. He'd sounded friendly as he'd questioned Manny after the tsunami.

Manny had rushed up to the official-looking Mr. Nomi and demanded he take action against Darby. By the time they'd finished talking though, Mr. Nomi had discovered Manny had disobeyed the evacuation order that might have saved his livestock.

"Super-duper," Mr. Nomi had said, as soon as he had enough information to arrest Cade's stepfather, and though Manny had struggled to free himself, Mr. Nomi had grinned and clicked a pair of handcuffs around his wrists.

Jonah introduced the other man to Kit as Mr. Klaus, and Darby thought he looked a lot like Santa Claus without a beard. He had wavy white hair, a flushed face, and a potbelly propped up by sturdy legs that ended in tightly laced hiking boots. But he sure didn't have merry Santa Claus eyes. His stern gaze probably didn't miss much.

For some reason, he made Darby nervous, but she remembered Jonah saying the ARC had been all over the island, searching for earthquake damage, so obviously Mr. Klaus's job demanded such watchfulness.

As Kit joined the group, crossing his arms and listening, Darby noticed Cade had slipped away with the horses and she did the same.

She untacked Navigator, picked up a hoof pick, and began cleaning mud from the gelding's hooves. Using the tip of the pick, she pried the mud away from the heel toward the toe just as Jonah had taught her so that she wouldn't push any grit into the sensitive part of the toe. She was glad to see that Navigator hadn't picked up any stones along the way.

As she worked, she eavesdropped, and wished she knew more about reservoirs, aquifers, ditches, and flumes. She only understood about half of what the men were talking about, although she was pretty sure they'd already tested 'Iolani's well and found it as pure as Jonah had insisted it would be.

"Mostly, the underground water is fine. The ponds and streams, they're polluted from all *da kine* storm wreckage," Mr. Nomi said.

As Darby put down the last hoof, she began grooming Navigator. *Da kine* was a pretty useful term, Darby thought, because it meant "that kind of thing." Mr. Nomi could mean everything from landslides that muddied the water to dead animals that tainted it.

Like Honi the pony drinking from the pond where the dead mongoose lay, Darby thought, but her alarm was interrupted by Navigator bumping against her, reminding her the currycomb felt as good as a massage and she should keep applying it to his sleek hide.

She smooched at the horse and kept brushing, even when Mr. Klaus spoke up.

"The county could have prevented some trouble."

"How's that?" Jonah asked.

"They've been turning a blind eye to people using unpurified water from ponds and streams instead of paying for municipal sources. Like the, uh, *neighborhood* above Crimson Vale."

One of the men cleared his throat. It sounded like Kit, but she didn't look over to see. It wasn't Kimo, and that's what really mattered, because Kimo and his father lived in one of the ramshackle houses that clustered on the lip of Crimson Vale.

Was it a poor neighborhood? It kind of looked that way, and Mr. Klaus was hinting that what these people had been taking for free might harm them.

The same thought must have occurred to Kit, because he asked, "Any illness there?"

"Not yet," Mr. Nomi said. "Or I guess I should say I'm not sure. It was the day before yesterday that we were up there, and Klaus is right. Not everyone'd be running in to a doctor to admit the water they've been borrowing is making them sick."

Day before yesterday, Darby had seen Tyson, Kimo's neighbor, in Ecology class, and he hadn't looked sick. He'd been malicious and mean, but no worse than usual. So there was probably no reason to worry about Kimo.

"Ours is still the biggest private well on the island, yeah?" Jonah asked, and the two men nodded. "We can share with neighbors if you can figure out how to do it."

"Thanks, Jonah," Mr. Nomi said, clapping him on the arm. "It's an iffy time to be trenching, but we'll keep your offer in mind."

"This must be the 'spirit of aloha' I've heard about," Mr. Klaus said.

"Klaus is from Utah," Mr. Nomi explained, but her grandfather brushed off the compliment.

"If I take care of my neighbors, comes a time when I'm in trouble, they might take care of me, yeah?"

Darby knew her grandfather wasn't just looking out for himself, but the men chuckled.

Just then, Cade walked by. He'd haltered Blue Ginger and was leading the mare while her foal followed.

"How's he doing?" Darby asked.

"I'd like to put 'em somewhere, so I can work," Cade said. "But where?"

Darby looked from the pigpen, past Hoku's corral, the old fox cages, the dog kennel, the round pen filled with cremello horses, and the half-fenced pasture. There were no other enclosures near Sun House, and if the foal was sick, he couldn't be put in with other horses.

"When Aunty Cathy gets home, maybe he can go into the office with her?" Darby suggested doubtfully.

"Gotta keep him moving," Cade said, but then his face brightened at the sound of a truck engine.

The Jeep, with patchy paint and no top but a roll bar, was a pretty distinctive vehicle. Driven by Cricket Pukai, it came down 'Iolani Ranch's dirt road and braked just short of the group of men.

Cade's disappointment showed. He'd been hoping it was Aunty Cathy, Darby thought, and that she'd learned something about his mother.

"She should be back soon," Darby said, but Cade kept his expression blank, as if he had no idea what she was talking about. He walked the mare and foal away from her.

"My sympathy's wasted on him," Darby whispered to Navigator, "but you like it, huh, boy?" She stroked the silken bay hide of the gelding's neck, and he blew through his lips, agreeing or relaxing, or both.

She left him tied to a metal ring, wearing nothing but a neck rope, and went toward the gathering in the driveway.

She might not know enough to participate in the water discussion, but curiosity about Cricket's role in the situation made it impossible for Darby to stay away.

Kit hid his grin an instant after it flashed at his girlfriend, but Darby could tell Cricket had seen it.

Kit had met Cricket at the feed store she managed. Though Kit had the easygoing ways of a Nevada buckaroo and Cricket was serious and brainy, always citing the latest studies and statistics in her crusade to protect animals, the two had just "clicked."

Kit made it clear that he admired Cricket's brainpower, but he couldn't help pestering her with jokes and compliments. It was obvious to everyone around them the unlikely pair had fun together.

Darby liked Cricket and respected the work she did as a rescue specialist with the Animal Rescue Society. According to Kit, Cricket had been insanely busy since the tsunami, and they saw each other most often when he drove to the Animal Rescue barn, where he was getting to know his wild mare, Medusa.

As usual, Cricket's black hair was piled into a messy bun. She pushed her thick glasses up the bridge of her nose, and her eyebrows arched. She intently followed the discussion before she even reached the men.

Darby waved at Cricket, but Cricket was too engrossed in the men's conversation to do anything but nod at Darby.

"Perfect timing," Mr. Nomi said as Cricket reached the group. "The Conservancy thinks the wild horses should be run up toward Sky Mountain as soon as possible."

Darby hung back across the half circle, hoping no one would notice her, even though she wished she could ask Mr. Nomi if he had Black Lava's herd confused with the wild bunch on Sky Mountain. The only wild horses he could be considering moving were the ones she'd watched on her high school field just yesterday. And they lived in Crimson Vale.

"What's the rush?" Cricket asked.

My role model, Darby thought. If those words had come out of *her* mouth, they would have sounded combative, but not from Cricket.

"To keep them away from the water," Mr. Nomi said.

Cricket seemed to be considering the proposal

when Mr. Klaus put in, "We'll be herding them with helicopters."

Darby caught a sharp breath. Her arms sprouted gooseflesh from long-ago cold and she heard it all again. Freezing, snowy winds howled to the thump of helicopter blades and the awful accompaniment of a horse screaming.

Chapter Six

Darby didn't realize she'd pressed her hands against her heart until Kit frowned at her. She let her arms fall back to her sides, but her pulse raced in her temples and wrists as she waited for someone to speak up for the horses.

"We have the personnel and the machines. Two experienced pilots have been doing disaster fly-overs," Mr. Klaus explained. He turned toward Cricket. "We can get this over and done with right away, and we hope your organization will back us up."

"You won't, will you?" Darby pleaded.

All eyes turned to her, until Cricket cleared her throat.

"I'm just a volunteer. I can't speak for the whole

organization," she explained, and Darby felt the unwelcome stares leave her until Cricket snapped her fingers as if she'd just remembered something and pointed. "Darby! That's right, you know something about wild horses and helicopters."

If only she could hole up like a prairie dog, Darby thought, but Cricket was already introducing her to Mr. Klaus and reminding Mr. Nomi where he'd seen Darby before.

Then, Cricket described how Mr. Nomi, representing the Department of Agriculture, and Mr. Klaus, from the Department of Health, worked together as part of the Agricultural Resource Conservation team.

"So, Darby, what bothers you about getting the wild horses to the mountains?" Mr. Nomi asked.

"Is it moving them or using helicopters that you don't like?" Mr. Klaus only gave her two choices.

"It's not that simple. There are wild horse herds up there already—"

"Proving it's a good wild horse habitat," Mr. Klaus cut in.

"There's another stallion up there, in charge. . . ." Darby's voice trailed off as she remembered the magnificent white stallion that had challenged Black Lava. But even as she said it, she knew he wasn't the biggest threat. "It's the helicopters. They're too dangerous." Darby forced the words around the shyness that was a roadblock between her brain and her tongue.

"We have experienced pilots," Mr. Klaus assured

her. "They fly over *volcanoes*, for heaven's sake, swooping low enough that volcanologists can carry out their work. I'm pretty sure that's much more dangerous than chasing horses."

"Not for the horses," she said.

Cricket and Kit exchanged a worried glance.

"She's thinking about what happened to her own horse, Hoku," Cricket said.

Darby nodded so hard her ponytail bounced, but Mr. Klaus still studied her and when he spoke again, his tone was condescending. "Would you rather have them down here, getting sick?"

A kaleidoscope of black manes, golden necks, red legs, and flowing silver tails spun in Darby's mind. None of them should ever turn dull-eyed and weak.

"Of course not," she snapped.

"That foal you just brought up is sick," Mr. Klaus argued. "If the domestic horses are ill, what chance will there be for the wild ones?"

Confused by the sympathy in Mr. Klaus's tone, Darby looked to Kit and asked, "Blue Moon's just colicky, right?"

"Seems so," Kit said.

That wasn't much help. Hadn't Kit seen helicopter and horse disasters back home in Nevada? Couldn't he imagine one? He was an adult, an experienced cowboy. *He* should be the one taking on these officials.

Mr. Nomi and Mr. Klaus returned to a discussion of running the horses to the mountains. In her frustration, Darby felt it was as if she hadn't spoken at all. But then Mr. Nomi asked Cricket, "What do *you* think about using helicopters for herding?"

"It's risky," Cricket said. "The sound and the wind of a chopper scare horses. They might stampede. Mares and foals might be separated. Foals might fall behind."

"You keep saying *might*," Mr. Klaus pointed out.

"Close monitoring by riders on horseback can prevent some of that," Cricket said, "but even excellent riders on the best domestic horses trying to stay with the herd under those conditions—it's tough."

"And with no one on the ground watching, mares break legs, foals get lost, and some horses get"—Darby searched for a word to describe her first sight of Hoku—"*brave* and try to outrun the helicopter, but end up running onto the street, right into the path of a bus. It's horrible."

"That would be a nightmare. But that's all it is, just a bad dream," Mr. Klaus said with a patronizing smile. "Don't you think you're making it sound worse than it is?"

"No, I'm not! My horse was hit by a bus back in Nevada while she was trying to escape a helicopter. She nearly died."

"This is Hawaii, not Nevada," Mr. Klaus replied.

Darby always tried to be respectful of adults, but Mr. Klaus wasn't making it easy.

She'd seen helicopter herding with her own eyes.

Why wouldn't he listen to her?

"Not all helicopters cause stampedes," Mr. Klaus continued.

"What about using a Judas horse, Darby?" Mr. Nomi asked.

Darby sensed he was trying to smooth things over and offer her a little respect.

"Well, I haven't actually seen that in action," she admitted, "but I know what you mean—using a tame horse to lead mustangs into a trap—"

Darby broke off. It would take time to train a tame horse to run up into the mountains. Even if they could do it fast enough, she couldn't picture Black Lava following along. In his equine mind, he was king.

She realized she was shaking her head dubiously when Mr. Nomi said, "Don't you think he'd follow a pretty mare?"

Like Hoku, Darby thought.

"Before the tsunami, I would have thought so," Darby said, "but I saw Black Lava plow through the waves, right past Hoku. He was so determined to get away from danger, I think he would have run my filly down if she hadn't moved out of his way. And there were the TV helicopters overhead. If he associated them with that day . . ." Darby took a deep breath, "No. I don't think it would work."

Cricket added, "That stallion knows his business."

But it wasn't Cricket that Mr. Klaus chuckled at. "You're quite the horse expert, aren't you, honey?"

There was no good answer. If she said yes, she sounded stuck-up. If she said no, why should they listen to her? Darby turned to her grandfather for help.

"Mr. Nomi, he asked my granddaughter's opinion, yeah?" Jonah gave an intense smile. "She's a polite girl, so she answered."

Mr. Klaus got her grandfather's point. The official had trespassed on tender territory and he knew it. He took a step backward before offering a sort of praise. "I guess you've been riding all your life."

If only he'd said, "I guess you've *loved* horses all your life," or "I guess horses have *fascinated* you all your life," Darby would have been proud to answer. But he hadn't, and Darby blushed so hard, her face hurt. She didn't want to admit that she'd just recently learned to ride.

"She's a natural. She has horses in her blood!"

When had Megan come down from the house? Darby had been so wrapped up in the conversation, she had no clue. But Megan had barged into the conversation just in time and she wanted to give her the world's biggest hug.

"How about this?" Cricket said suddenly. "Why not use the 'Iolani Ranch paniolos to herd mustangs the old-fashioned way, on horseback?"

"That's crazy talk," Jonah said with a bark of laughter.

"It might work," Kit said.

Anyone within a mile could have recognized the

excitement in Kit's and Jonah's expressions. They were both up for the challenge.

"Don't count on Kimo," Megan put in. "That's what I came down to tell you. He called to say he and his dad have 'a bug.' I don't know what kind," Megan said before anyone could ask, "but he sounded awful."

"So, that would mean Kit, Cade, me," Cricket said, "and Jonah?"

"I'll chance 'em," Jonah said. "But if you don't need me right now—" His quick glance took in Darby as well as Kit and Cricket. "I want to go look at that colt."

As Mr. Klaus and Mr. Nomi shook hands with Jonah and promised to stay in touch, Megan offered, "Darby and I can help."

"We'll talk about that," Cricket said, glancing after Jonah.

"And maybe my mom," Megan volunteered. "She's recovered from her concussion, and that's almost one of us for each wild horse."

"That's what we'd need," Cricket said, but she looked dubious.

The two officials didn't notice. They were consulting a spiral-bound notebook and a map.

Cricket edged closer to Kit and whispered, "Do you think Darby's ready?"

In that moment, Kit's eyes showed all his misgivings.

Darby knew wild horses were unpredictable. They'd

spread out, then stick together: they'd gallop over hills, then veer around them. And the terrain might require jumping, quick decisions, and just plain luck to stick in the saddle.

But Kit only said, "That's hard riding."

"If she's not up to it, we won't take chances."

Mr. Klaus could have at least looked up from the map, Darby thought.

He didn't even glance at her as he said, "If we used an inexperienced rider in a government-sponsored wildlife relocation we'd be leaving ourselves open to a lawsuit."

Is he refusing to let me ride because I disagreed with him over the helicopters? Darby thought so, but she couldn't brag that she'd ridden Hoku, a barely trained mustang, at a flat-out gallop in the midst of a volcanic eruption.

Even I can't believe that, Darby thought wryly, *and I was there!*

But she wanted to go. She wanted to feel like part of a wild horse herd. She wanted to make sure the wild horses weren't mistreated. And, though it wasn't a very mature motive, she wanted to show Mr. Klaus that while he might be a big shot at the Department of Health, he wasn't the boss on this ranch.

"You wouldn't leave me out, would you, Kit?" she asked, and when the foreman looked pained, she added, "It's not like I'm going to sue the ranch."

"Not the ranch, the federal government," Mr. Klaus corrected her. "As government representatives, we couldn't allow that, could we, Mike?" He turned to Mr. Nomi.

"Kit?" Darby insisted, before a startled Mr. Nomi could reply.

"That's up to the boss," Kit reminded her.

Mr. Klaus looked from Darby to Kit, let out a deep exhalation of annoyance, then gulped the last inch of cold coffee from his cup.

"Thanks," he said, handing the empty mug to Kit.

He's the ranch foreman. He's a bronc rider. He's the oldest son of a Native American family, not a waiter, Darby thought. She felt insulted for Kit.

"Thanks for your time. All of you," Mr. Nomi said. He smiled politely at Cricket, Kit, and Megan, but it felt to Darby like his eyes purposely skimmed past her. He headed for the car, saying, "Talk to you soon."

She felt self-conscious. She'd obviously made Mr. Nomi think less of her. When Mr. Klaus pulled open the car door, he glanced back at them and chuckled. "Think about using helicopters," he said. "Most would say they're more efficient than kids playing cowgirl."

Chapter Seven

Kids playing cowgirl!

Resentment flashed through Darby's entire body.

She turned to Kit and Cricket, pretty sure they'd stop being so nice now that the two men had left.

But neither of them said a word. In the quiet, she heard nearby hooves. Blue Ginger and Blue Moon thudded along with grudging patience, while Hoku's hooves danced eagerly as she kept watch to figure out what the other horses were doing.

At least, that's how Darby heard them. For the thousandth time, she realized she was a lot more sensitive and sensible when it came to horses. If only she were half as good with people.

Something was wrong in the slow-motion way Kit

eased off his black Stetson, showing even blacker hair, then rubbed the back of his neck. He was choosing his words carefully.

"You blew it bad, *keiki*," Kit said.

"*I* did?" Darby squeaked. That was the opposite of what she'd expected to hear.

Whose side are you on? Darby wondered, but she didn't ask.

"I got as healthy a distrust of strangers—'specially those workin' for the government—as anyone, but you missed a good chance to keep quiet and let things roll out the way they were meant to."

"But . . ." Darby glanced at Megan for support and saw the older girl's discomfort.

So, Megan wasn't on her side, either.

Darby took a deep breath. She felt a cold stab in her chest. She was relieved when Megan gestured vaguely toward Sun House and left.

Kit wasn't going anywhere, though. He was brushing dust from his hat brim. Three knuckles showed torn skin and dried blood. He must have more to say.

"Those guys liked the look of our well. They didn't order any extreme conservation measures, and they could've. They didn't insist a vet come out and look at Blue Moon. They trusted us to take care of business."

One thing she'd learned from Samantha Forster and Mrs. Allen in Nevada was that ranchers prided themselves on being independent and self-sufficient. Jonah and his cowboys were no different, and Mr.

Nomi and Mr. Klaus knew it.

For the first time since the men had left, Kit looked up at her.

Darby nodded, but she *knew* she'd been right about one thing.

"What about the helicopters?" Darby folded her arms. "I've seen what can happen. There's no way I could keep quiet."

"You started out pretty good," Kit told her. "Their idea wasn't great, but they would've come around—"

"They *did* come around," Cricket said quietly. "And if they hadn't, I would have reminded them of that crash in Wyoming." She looked aside at Kit and said, "A pilot herding wild horses failed to maintain proper altitude."

Cricket was right. An example like that, one that showed concern for people as well as horses, would have been more persuasive.

You started out pretty good, Kit had said, but Mr. Klaus had ended their conversation by joking that she was a kid playing cowgirl.

Darby knew how she'd made her good beginning go wrong. Embarrassed—no, humiliated!—she replayed her whining about not being included.

That had zero to do with protecting Black Lava's herd. She'd sounded like a kid, all right.

Besides, *nothing* would convince Kit or Jonah to let her go along on the horse drive if they had qualms about her riding ability.

And yet Darby only considered running for her bedroom, to hide, for a fraction of a second.

"What should I do?" she asked Kit.

"What I'm going to do is go take a look at that foal," Cricket said. "We have a few sick horses at the barn. With luck, this baby's symptoms won't be similar."

Role model, Darby thought again as she gazed after Cricket.

Alone with Kit now, Darby blurted, "Are you mad at me?"

It seemed like forever before Kit shook his head no.

"Surprised," he admitted. "You usually think ahead, act sensible, yeah?"

Kit grinned at his Hawaiian-sounding sentence, but his eyes turned wise.

Too wise, Darby thought, for a guy in his twenties.

"Know what my grandpa Mac used to say at times like this?"

"No," she whispered, "but I bet I won't like it."

Kit matched her lopsided smile, then made his pronouncement.

"Listen, or your tongue will make you deaf." Kit stayed quiet as the whir of bird wings passed overhead and the slosh of Navigator drinking at the tack-room trough drifted in to underline what he'd said.

Darby memorized the words.

Listen, or your tongue will make you deaf was a better saying than *Shut up so you can hear what other people are saying.* And she needed to learn that, because even though she'd been too shy to speak up for most of her life, Hawaii seemed to be changing her.

Or she was changing in Hawaii.

"Don't get too down on yourself before you help me dump the water barrels."

"Okay," Darby agreed, "but what's your grandfather's name again?"

"MacArthur Ely," Kit answered proudly. "He's the best."

Darby followed Kit toward the barrels, but her mind was elsewhere.

She'd been thinking about adding a chapter to her diary called "Paniolo Wisdom," but this meant she had to change the title. She might be able to say *Kit* was part buckaroo and part paniolo but not his Shoshone grandfather.

But she'd have to solve that problem later. Tipping water from the barrels she and Megan had set out last night, into Hoku's trough and the water troughs by the tack room, kept Darby focused on lifting and balancing and trying not to get too wet.

With that chore finished, Kit told Darby to lead each cremello up to the tack room to drink while he walked Cricket to her Jeep, so she could get back to work at the feed store.

Hoku objected by slamming her corral fence with jealous kicks.

Afraid the filly would splinter the wood, Darby shouted, "You know I love you best!"

Though Darby couldn't see Jonah from where she stood, she heard him moan, "Enough!"

Darby had latched the last cremello back into the round pen when Aunty Cathy pulled up and got out of the Land Rover, arms full of grocery bags and a big flat box.

"Let me help," Darby said, jogging over as Aunty Cathy managed to slam the truck door with her hip.

"Just take the box." Aunty Cathy blew her bangs out of her eyes, then added, "It's for you."

"What did your doctor say?" Darby asked as she maneuvered the box out of Aunty Cathy's grasp.

"My concussion's a thing of the past. I'm cleared for duty," Aunty Cathy said.

"Oh, good—hey! This is the saddle blanket I ordered for Hoku!" Darby whooped, finally recognizing the return address on the package.

She'd used a little of her reward money from finding Stormbird, the lost cremello colt, to buy Hoku a saddle blanket she'd been admiring in a horse gear catalog.

Although Hoku wasn't ready for a saddle yet, Darby couldn't resist.

She stopped right in the middle of the ranch yard to open the cardboard box. As she struggled to rip loose the tape, Darby realized Cade had come to watch.

"Show us," Aunty Cathy said and then, as Darby

pulled the blanket free of its wrappings, she added, "Oh, Darby, it will look perfect on her."

"Totally," said Megan, who'd just jogged down the stairs to take a grocery bag from her mother.

"Yeah," Darby said. She gave the blanket a flip, admiring it.

Bright with sun colors—from yellow-gold to flame-orange—it was worth every penny she'd spent.

When the filly gave a lonesome neigh, Aunty Cathy took pity on her and said, "I guess you should show her what she got."

Just then, Darby realized Megan was looking past her at Cade.

Cade had drawn himself up to his full height. His arms were locked gunfighter-ready at his sides. He hadn't come to watch her open the parcel. He waited to learn if Aunty Cathy had learned anything about his mother.

"Cade, I don't have much news for you." Aunty Cathy's voice was matter-of-fact. "But Peg at the grocery store saw her yesterday, so she's definitely—safe."

Cade nodded.

With three pairs of eyes watching, he showed no reaction except that his fingers closed against his palms.

"Mahalo," he managed. "Really, thanks a lot."

"Of course." Aunty Cathy sounded sweet and motherly and maybe that was more than he could take, because Cade turned and walked away.

"Just great," Megan snapped, but she waited until Cade was out of earshot to say more. "All this time, he's been imagining the worst, thinking she's drowned or trapped or—and she hasn't come to see if *he's* okay. If I had a mother like her, I wouldn't be searching for her. I'd hide!"

With that, Megan gave Aunty Cathy's cheek a quick kiss. Then, she ran after Cade.

Darby's jolt of surprise was seconded by Aunty Cathy as she said, "I wish I'd seen *that* coming."

"What do you think she'll say to him?" Darby asked.

"I don't imagine there's anything he wants to hear from anyone," Aunty Cathy said. Shaking her head, Aunty Cathy gave Darby a half smile, then headed for Sun House.

Darby folded the blanket back into its box and carried it under one arm.

Chain links jingled across the grass as Francie the goat came as far as she could toward Darby. Francie's bleat of greeting made Darby stop.

"How are you, little girl?" she asked. She kneaded the bony top of the goat's head and looked after Megan, though she'd disappeared near the bunkhouse. "I hope Megan knows what she's doing, don't you?"

Francie nuzzled the front of Darby's shirt, then tasted it.

"That's for wearing, not eating," she told the goat, but Francie had already reached the same conclusion.

Kimo's dad had given Francie to Jonah as a joke. She was a fainting goat, a breed rumored to have been created by shepherds to pass out under stress. That way, if a wolf or coyote was on the prowl, the valuable sheep would flee, leaving the unconscious goat for the predators.

Darby hated that idea. Still, she teased Francie. "Maybe you've got the right idea. If I'd fainted at the mention of herding with helicopters, I wouldn't have been able to run my mouth and make people think I was a *child*."

Naaa, Francie bleated, but Darby didn't try to interpret the comment. She just kissed the goat's silky head before getting a better grip on the box, then jogged off to show Hoku her present.

Two months ago, she probably would have just whipped the blanket out of its box to display it for Hoku. Now she knew the action might scare the filly, so she knelt outside the corral, opened the box so that the blanket showed, and scooted the box under the bottom fence rail.

If Hoku wanted to investigate it, she could.

In the meantime, Darby took down the halter and tangerine-striped rope from where she'd slung them over the top fence rail. Hoku knew them and associated them with good things—like going somewhere with Darby—so Darby went into the corral and haltered her horse.

"Yep, that's for you," Darby said when Hoku rolled

her eyes toward the box.

Darby walked over and lifted out the blanket.

No spatter of gravel or explosion of dust came from her horse's hooves. She didn't shy or show the whites of her eyes in fear, so Darby approached the filly with the blanket draped over her arms. She stopped a few feet away, not forcing her filly to examine the blanket, just offering the new object for inspection.

"Hoku, it's for you," she said.

The filly sniffed the blanket. She tasted it. She listened as Darby flapped it.

"You're such a big girl," she said, and then she made a quick kissing sound.

Hoku shook her head, spilling her golden mane to one side of her neck, then the other. After that, the filly looked into Darby's eyes with pure acceptance.

"What did I do to earn that?" Darby whispered to her horse, but she knew the answer. She was kind. She cared. She paid attention.

Right now, for instance, Hoku's ears stood straight up. About the size of Darby's hand, with all four fingers and her thumb aligned, the sorrel's ears were alert. Hoku gave back the attention Darby lavished on her.

"You're not afraid of this silly blanket, are you?"

Hoku's ears changed. They cupped to catch each word. The filly stood so still, Darby saw past the fine golden fringe edging each ear to the dark pink skin and the filigree of veins leading to Hoku's heart.

Darby didn't know how long they'd stood together

before she realized she was humming to her horse. It took a few seconds more for the lyrics to emerge.

"When you wish upon a star, makes no difference who you are." Darby didn't know all of the words, but it didn't matter.

Darby sighed with pleasure, then she began gliding the blanket over Hoku's back, neck, and face. The filly nipped and sniffed and nuzzled.

"So much for horse charming," Darby told the filly. "You're the magic maker."

Or maybe they'd hypnotized each other, and that was why Darby decided to ride Hoku—not Navigator—on her first trip to Patrick Zink's house when Jonah came by to tell her Patrick had called earlier, begging for company.

 Chapter Eight

The Zink family owned the acreage that adjoined 'Iolani Ranch to the south. It had once been an old sugar plantation that stretched from the grasslands into the rain forest.

The sugar mill had long ago fallen into ruin. It was overgrown with vines, though the house next door, which Darby had only glimpsed down its long drive-way when they drove by, appeared modern.

The Zink property had been bordered with a barbed wire fence until Darby had become friends with Patrick Zink and let slip Jonah's poor opinion of barbed wire. Now, expensive white wooden fencing enclosed the neighboring acreage.

Patrick Zink was in the eighth grade with her at

Lehua High, but she hadn't gotten to know him until she and her mom took a ride to the old sugar plantation.

Darby smiled as she remembered Patrick's pith helmet. She hadn't known that anyone wore those hats outside of movies, but there he'd been, in real life, exploring the ruins of the old place.

Soon Darby found out he loved books as much as she did, and he had an encyclopedic knowledge of the island's history, especially the A-Z Sugar Plantation that had once been run by the Acosta and Zink families.

Darby had only talked with Patrick twice since the ugly accident that had peeled off the top layer of skin on his leg. During their first conversation, Patrick said the doctors had referred to that part of his injury as "degloving." Though she didn't consider herself squeamish, Darby thought that was an unsettlingly accurate description.

As she and Hoku neared the driveway to the Zink house, they looked both ways, then crossed the street to walk in the shade of ohia trees, which grew closer together on the Zinks' side of the street.

Darby was enjoying the red blossoms and salty sea air, when she heard a horse nicker.

Hoku halted suddenly and sniffed, trying to locate the other horse by scent. When that didn't work, Hoku stood soundless, listening for the other horse. When the nicker didn't come again, Hoku snorted, asking the other horse to come out.

And she did.

A beautiful black-and-white paint stretched her nose out from behind a tree at the edge of the Zinks' driveway. Then, she emerged completely.

Mistwalker was masked by satiny black from muzzle to eye patches. Her flat cheeks, forehead, and neck were white, but she had a long, graceful, black throat and body, and her black mane fell in tendrils.

"That's Patrick's horse," she told Hoku, "but what's she doing here?"

Just like Honi, Patrick's paint mare was allowed to roam free, and Darby had mixed feelings about the horses' liberty. Although this end of Moku Lio Hihiu wasn't heavily inhabited, the streets had their share of cars.

Darby looked around for Patrick. Even with a walking cast, he probably couldn't go too far from the house, so it was no surprise she didn't see him, but when Darby turned her gaze back to Mistwalker, she realized the mare was acting strange.

The first time she and her mother had encountered the paint, they'd thought she was a wild horse. They'd realized their mistake when Mistwalker came to greet them. Clearly friendly and tame, the mare had nuzzled Navigator and nosed Ellen's arm, but now the paint mare kept her distance.

Darby clucked softly to the horse, then called, "Come here, girl."

Mistwalker threw back her forelock, neighed, and pawed the ground.

Hoku answered the mare's summons by trotting forward.

Riding along the roadside hadn't been one of her best ideas, Darby decided. Hoku ignored the impact of asphalt on her unshod hooves as she followed Mistwalker along the edge of the street.

Mistwalker looked back at Hoku, snorting and urging the filly to come closer, but each time they drew near, Mistwalker moved faster.

What did she want?

Then, Darby saw Patrick.

Sprawled in a folding chair next to a beach umbrella, he sat at the edge of the driveway. His eyes were shut beneath his round black-rimmed glasses. His face was an unnatural shade of pink that made the freckles across his nose and cheeks stand out. His khaki pants were cut short on the right to accommodate his cast, but the full-length left pant leg was smeared with mud. His pith helmet lay nearby, on the ground.

What have you been up to? Darby wondered.

Patrick had a reputation for being clumsy and accident-prone, but wouldn't his parents be more watchful because of his injury?

Darby felt a quick flash of guilt. The last time she'd talked to Patrick, he'd told her how bored he was and how he longed to meet Hoku. She'd promised to ride over and visit, but that had been almost a week ago.

"Patrick?" Darby leaned forward, cheek resting against Hoku's vanilla silk mane.

She spoke softly, afraid to spook either of the horses.

Patrick didn't move. Was he breathing? Logically, she knew he was. Still, his accident had been serious, and it was fresh in her memory.

Darby dismounted slowly, keeping her hold on Hoku's rein as she walked to Patrick's side. The front of his faded green T-shirt rose and fell. Of course he was breathing.

"Patrick," she said, "wake up."

She shook his shoulders but he didn't rouse.

She looked at Hoku, as if the wild filly could help, and Patrick chose that moment to sit up with a snort.

Both horses threw their heads high and widened their eyes in alarm, but neither bolted.

"Hey! Darby, hi!" Patrick said, groggy but ecstatic.

"Are you okay?" she asked.

"Sure," Patrick answered. "How about you?"

"I think my heart stopped, but other than that, I'm fine," Darby told him.

"Wow, this is your Hoku!"

"Yep, my Hoku," Darby echoed proudly, but she was amazed at her filly's reaction to Patrick. Hoku was watchful and braced to bolt, but she didn't flatten her ears and glare as she did with most males.

"That white marking on her chest is just as you described it, like a white sea star." Patrick's voice was gruffer than usual. As if a few cobwebs of sleep still hung on, he cleared his throat loudly and addressed the horse. "I'm overjoyed to meet you, Hoku, but I won't look into your beautiful wild eyes. . . ." Patrick purposely switched his gaze to Darby.

Could Hoku trust Patrick because he was seated? Or had she received some sort of equine endorsement from Mistwalker?

"What are you doing out here?" Darby asked.

"This is the best place to get some company, since I couldn't go to school and now, of course, it's closed."

"You are keeping up on the news," Darby congratulated him.

"I do my best, since my parents won't drive me anyplace. They order me to rest, but that's not easy when I'm not allowed to do anything to get tired. I saw Tutu, though."

"Out here?" Darby asked.

Patrick nodded. "She rode Prettypaint over, because she needed a book she'd loaned me."

"I didn't know you were friends with Tutu," Darby said.

"I think everyone is," Patrick said.

He was right. Her great-grandmother was an honored elder, a wisewoman, and a skilled herbalist.

Darby hadn't met anyone who didn't call her Tutu, as though she was great-grandmother to everyone on the island.

"I was talking to her when Kimo drove up this morning, on his way to work at your place," Patrick went on. "And you know what happened? He pulled the truck over, got out, and before he said anything, passed out right there."

Patrick pointed a few feet away, where Mistwalker stood, nibbling the sparse roadside grass.

"Kimo passed out?" Darby gasped.

Kimo was a big, tough cowboy. Since her first day on the island, she'd thought of him as square and hard as a stone house. How could something, especially something invisible, like a germ, knock him down and out?

"It's difficult to imagine, isn't it?" Patrick sympathized.

"But Tutu helped him?"

"Of course," Patrick said, but then Mistwalker nuzzled the nape of his neck. He shivered and almost tipped over his chair before he went on. "When Kimo regained consciousness, she gave him something from that cloth sack. You know, the one she carries in front of her, when she rides Prettypaint? Then she shooed Kimo back into his truck and told him to go back home and let his father take care of him."

"They're both sick," Darby said. "Kimo called the ranch and talked to Megan."

Darby thought of the students collapsing in the school office, of Blue Moon, and now Kimo and his father.

"What are you thinking about?" Patrick asked.

Because she admired his clever mind full of facts, Darby told him what she and Ann had seen at school. Then, she asked, "Do you think everyone on the island has the same thing?"

"It's rare for illnesses to jump from one species to the other," Patrick mused.

"Tutu mentioned that she'd seen stomach upset accompanied by a high fever after flooding before. She blamed it on bad water. Possibly animals have different, but equally negative, reactions to post-storm pollution."

While Patrick was lost in his thoughts, Darby compared his opinion—and Tutu's—to those of her Ecology teacher, Mr. Silva; Mr. Nomi; and Mr. Klaus.

"Hey, I didn't even ask how *you're* feeling." Darby squatted in the shade of the beach umbrella, still holding Hoku's rein.

"Pretty well, thanks. I had a terrible night though. I believe the skin is regenerating. Tutu discussed it with me, and she's sure the discomfort will pass soon," he said, then smiled. "What a kind woman she is."

"Very kind," Darby agreed.

She fought down the urge to smile. Something about Patrick amused her, but in a good way. He spoke a little like she imagined a college professor would, and he was interested in everything. She felt lucky to have him as a friend.

"What was the book you borrowed from Tutu?" she asked.

"*The Complete Treasury of Herbal Medicine*," Patrick said. "It's fascinating. It's thick as a loaf of bread, with a cracked leather cover and no copyright date. It looks very old."

"Hey! While you've been sitting here watching the world go by, have you seen Cade's mother?"

"No, though I'm not certain I'd recognize her," Patrick said. "Was she lost in the tsunami?"

"Lost, but not, you know, drowned or anything," Darby said, and then she told Patrick how she and Cade had gone to find Dee. She described Dee's beloved pony and Cade's certainty that Dee was still on the island even before his hunch was verified by Aunty Cathy.

"Half Welsh, half Arab, and she's named Honi the pony." He chuckled at the rhyme, but then his expression sharpened, and Darby sensed Patrick was going into junior detective mode. "Was she all right?"

"She was perky and plump, but that was no thanks to Dee."

Darby stopped, scolding herself for being critical of a woman she didn't know. But she'd gone this far, she thought, so she told Patrick about Honi's taste for water lilies.

"She can't seem to get enough of them," Darby said. "She kept one in her mouth even when she was galloping up to the house."

Darby was smiling at the memory, when Patrick asked, "Wait, she was eating water lilies straight out of the pond? In the area they won't allow the wild horses back into?"

Darby closed her eyes and pictured sunlight illuminating the muddy waters full of death and debris.

Then, she pictured the serene pond where the pony had stood. Was the altitude the same? Had tsunami waters washed over that pond?

Think hard, she told herself, because a lot could depend on the ugly memory, including Honi's life.

 Chapter Nine

"How did the pond look?" Patrick insisted.

"Pretty," Darby said. "Like a pond. Don't get frustrated with me, Patrick," she said when he rolled his eyes. "I don't come from a place where there are lots of ponds. But I did see something interesting there. My first ever mongoose. Even if he was dead—"

"If you'd grown up here, you'd have seen plenty of them," Patrick assured her. "Even though they're not native. In fact, they weren't brought to Hawaii until the 1800s. A Hawaiian sugar farmer heard the boast of a Cuban sugar plantation owner that the mongoose could successfully control his rodent population, but it turned out, as with so many other non-native species, they had no natural enemies here."

Patrick stopped. He didn't seem to have run out of breath. He looked more like he was waiting for her to say something.

"So you see my point?" he encouraged her.

"No."

"What would kill a mongoose?"

"Cade and I assumed it drowned."

"Perhaps," Patrick said, "but the mongoose is descended from the early civet. It swims."

"Nothing could swim in that wall of water," Darby pointed out.

"Of course you're right," he agreed. "Still, it would be worthwhile to have the water in that pond tested for contaminants."

"Honi."

Darby didn't need to say more.

"If she was eating water lilies there, she was ingesting the water, too. Directly or via the plants," Patrick said. His hands fidgeted and his left knee jiggled with contained energy. "If only we could go up and get her out of there."

"Cade and I thought of doing that," Darby said, "but just in case Honi was sick, we didn't want to bring her back to the ranch."

Why hadn't she told Mr. Klaus and Mr. Nomi? They'd been right there at the ranch. They would have been able to test the pony, the water, and if there was trouble, they would have known what to do about it.

Why had it taken Patrick to make her realize the danger was real?

She must have looked scared.

"It's only a theory," Patrick said. "It's not sound science to jump to any conclusions. Still, if she were my pony . . ."

Feeling Darby's agitation even before she bolted to her feet, Hoku stepped back, eyes wide.

"Can I get you anything before I leave?" Darby offered, but she was thinking, *Please don't say yes.*

"No. I'm fine. Do you have to go right now?"

"I think so," she replied. "I'd better find Cade or someone who can help me catch Honi."

"And then—?" Patrick broke off and Darby was glad. He didn't have to be a mind reader to know she didn't have a plan beyond saving the pony from dying alone.

Thirty minutes later, Darby wished more than anything that she wasn't riding Hoku. In another second, she would have turned left toward Sun House, but Dee's dusky pony picked that instant to bound out of the clearing she'd been grazing in and head toward the taro fields.

"You little beast," she muttered, but she gave Hoku her head and rode high on the filly's neck as the mustang chased after the curiously small horse.

A leaf with sawtooth edges slapped across Darby's brow.

This was such a bad idea. Almost any horse on the island would have stronger immunities than Hoku.

On the other hand, Honi wasn't acting like a sick animal.

Probably I'm imagining it, Darby thought, but Honi seems to be delighted by this wild pony chase.

Before she knew it, they were at the pond.

But Honi wasn't.

Hoku snorted. Her hooves stuttered in place as she waited for the pony to rematerialize, but Honi didn't. And when Hoku started toward the pond, Darby fought her.

"No way!" Darby pulled her rope rein tight enough that her filly was even more confused.

Hoku couldn't be very thirsty. Darby had filled her trough and watched her drink from it only a few hours ago. Just the same, Darby hoped it wouldn't come to a struggle. Without a bit, she couldn't win, so she'd have to depend on the filly's desire to please her.

Hoku came to something that was almost a stop. She seemed to be making up her mind, so Darby helped her.

"Hey, baby," she said, placing her hand on the filly's sorrel neck. "I'm doing this for your own good." Hoku's snort rocked them both. "Yeah, that argument doesn't work for me, either," she told her horse. "But you're barely warm, and I don't know what's in that water, so you can forget about having any of it."

As if she wanted to remove temptation from her

view, Hoku lifted her front hooves and pivoted away from the pond.

As she did, Darby saw Manny's truck in front of the house perched above the taro field.

Manny was in jail, but before he'd been sent there he'd claimed that Dee had stolen his truck. So, that meant Dee was there.

If she could report to Cade that she'd seen his mother with her own eyes . . .

"Let's go," Darby said, and Hoku didn't hesitate.

As they drew closer Darby saw why Hoku was willing to trot toward a place that had to hold bad memories from the tsunami.

Joker was tied to a post supporting the roof over the front porch.

Darby let Hoku advance to touch noses with Joker, but she didn't call out to Cade.

"Well, what do you want from me?" a woman's voice asked. "I figured you were fine. You live on that big fancy ranch now. You have everything you need over there, don't you?"

Cade might have welcomed an interruption, but Darby didn't know how to break into the argument.

"You could have let me know you were—" Cade broke off and revised what he'd been about to say. "*Where* you were. I haven't heard a single word from you since the tsunami."

"Yeah, well, in case you haven't heard, my husband's in jail. *Jail.* I've had my hands full taking care of this place alone. Look at this house! It's all busted up from the quake. Oh, what do you care."

Darby rolled her eyes. Poor Cade! Dee was clearly trying to guilt-trip him.

Cade stepped out of the house. Arms folded in anger, he didn't look surprised to see Darby.

Exhaling forcefully, Cade let her know he hated the smell of cigarette smoke that had followed him out. He also looked wary, as if he was waiting for her to say the wrong thing.

"Want to go?" Darby asked.

Before he could answer, the door behind him opened, revealing a woman Darby recognized from the awards ceremony. Dee stood leaning in the doorway, clutching her cigarette. She had straggly, unwashed blond hair and was surprisingly tall and broad-shouldered for a woman who had been too afraid of her husband to stand up to him. Back before hard living and disappointment had etched unhappy lines in her face and blotted the light from her eyes, she might have had the good looks Cade had now.

"You gonna introduce me to your girlfriend?" she asked.

"Darby is Jonah's granddaughter," he told her.

"We saw Honi and I—" Darby began.

"How do you know Honi?" Dee interrupted.

"Cade and I saw her the other day, and I've been thinking it might not be such a good idea for her to be eating the water lilies and drinking out of the pond."

As Darby explained what she knew about the polluted water, Dee's face took on an unreadable expression. Did she resent Darby's interest in her pony or was Darby adding one more worry to Dee's endless list?

"Honi is fine," Dee said.

Cade and Darby exchanged glances. No one could know that just by looking at the pony.

"Maybe a vet could take a look at her," Darby suggested.

"Right," Dee said. "No vet's going to come out here. Even if one did, tests are expensive, and a vet couldn't just eyeball Honi and see if something's wrong inside."

Worry marked deep lines between Dee's brows, but talk of Honi seemed to have changed the atmosphere and made Dee less defensive.

A smile flicked across her face and just as quickly disappeared. "Listen, Cade. I'm glad you're here. There's something I need to talk to you about."

"I can go," Darby offered. Dee made it sound like a family matter.

"Stay," Cade insisted.

Maybe he didn't want to be alone if Dee was about to confide some illegal thing Manny had done or how she might be involved in it.

A look of annoyance flashed over Dee's face, but she chased it away with another quick smile.

"I guess there's no reason she can't hear this," she said. "All right, here's the thing: If you leave Jonah and come back here to live with me, I'll put half the land in your name when you're sixteen."

Darby stared at the toes of her faded maroon boots. Cade loved his mother. Didn't Dee know that? Why did she think she had to use bribery to make him come home?

Cade stayed quiet, and Dee must have thought her offer hadn't been good enough, because she continued. "As soon as I get back on my feet, we can get cattle and horses."

"Mom." Cade's voice was dull, emotionless.

"Think of it," Dee urged him. "You could have your own ranch."

Cade kept his expression blank, but when he glanced over his shoulder, past the ruined taro field to the green grass and soaring sea cliffs beyond, Darby saw the dreams he was trying to ignore.

Dee was getting to him. The promise of his own ranch was too wonderful to push aside. Darby understood that, but what if it was a hollow offer? Dee might just want him back to do all the work around the place.

"So? What do you think?" Dee pressed Cade for an answer.

You think she's crazy! Darby wanted to give Cade's shoulder a punch to distract him, but she didn't. She kept her lips pressed together, locking her opinion inside.

Listen, or your tongue will make you deaf, she reminded herself, but Darby was only doing it in the hope that

Cade would see through his mother, not because she thought Dee would say anything of value.

"I don't know," Cade said slowly. "Things around here would have to change."

"Like how?" Dee asked.

"Like you'd have to get a legal divorce from Manny," he said firmly, "and you'd have to get a job."

"What kind of job could I possibly get?" Dee asked. Her tone bordered on anger. "All I've ever done was take care of you, cook, clean, and help Manny work the taro fields, and now look at them! Ruined by that flood. Besides, why would I need a job?"

"The cattle and horses, remember? How can that happen if you're not working?"

"Jonah Kealoha doesn't pay you?" Dee asked, darting a quick look at Darby.

"Not in dollars," Cade said, and there was a stubborn pride in his words that warned Dee not to criticize his mentor.

"Okay." She gave in. "I'll go out and see what I can find, but it might take a while and it would be easier if you were here to look after things while I'm job hunting."

"Nuh-uh," Cade said. "I'll come back once you have the job and have kept it for a while."

"What's a while?" Dee's eyes narrowed.

"Long enough to have money in the bank—*some* money, anyway."

"If I do that, you'll come back?" Dee checked.

"And if you divorce Manny," he reminded her.

Looking gloomy, she shook her head. "That won't happen overnight, either."

Then you'd better get started, Darby thought, but she couldn't have said it to her own mother. In fact, she thought, letting her eyes slide to the side to assess Cade, where was he getting the nerve to confront his mom like this?

"This will be really good for both of us," Dee said suddenly. She tossed away her cigarette and used both hands to smooth her hair back from her face.

For the first time, Darby thought it might work.

After all, her own mother had left home for good, and now she and Darby's grandfather were piecing their relationship back together. Of course, neither her mother nor Jonah had been as irresponsible as Dee. Still, Cade loved his mother, and Dee was showing a glimmer of affection for her son.

Even ugly problems between a parent and child should probably be patched up, shouldn't they? Darby thought.

"Mom? There's one more thing," Cade added. He walked toward Joker, keeping his back to Dee. "You'd have to quit the cigarettes."

Yes! Darby thought. *Go, Cade!*

"Aw, come on, son—"

"You only started after you married Manny."

"But it's been years," Dee complained.

Cade stuck his foot in his stirrup and swung onto Joker. He was looking down, evening out his reins, and that was when Darby saw his hands shaking. Cade's bravado was costing him something, but Dee couldn't possibly guess that by the way he shrugged.

"Either you want me to come back or you don't."

"I do, Cade." Dee said it quickly, firmly. "I want you to come back home. That's *one* thing you can count on."

Darby couldn't tell if Cade believed her or not, because he didn't answer. He just flashed his hand in a sort of wave.

Besides, Darby was paying close attention to her horse. She didn't have to ask Hoku to back up. The filly was ready to leave.

Right now.

 Chapter Ten

Riding home, they didn't talk much.

When they neared the pond, Darby asked, "Should we try to find Honi before it gets dark?"

"Nope," he said curtly.

Darby didn't ask what Cade was thinking and, at first, she didn't share her own thoughts, even though her mind was churning and full.

She wanted to tell Cade he could not leave 'Iolani Ranch. He'd be leaving them shorthanded. He'd be giving up his study of paniolo ways. It would make her grandfather sad. It would be like throwing Jonah's affection and protection back in his face, even if Jonah understood why Cade was going.

"Jonah would miss you," Darby said.

"Same here," Cade snapped, then he extended Joker's trot so that Hoku was no longer even with the Appaloosa's shoulder but with his rump.

And Darby couldn't see Cade's face.

"Huh." She breathed out a mix of frustration and admiration.

A few minutes later, she began wondering if there was another reason Cade would consider moving—something besides his longing to reconnect with his mother.

Cade knew cattle and horses because Jonah had taught him well, and Cade probably wanted to make ranching his life's work. But because he was not Jonah's biological son, did he think he stood no chance of inheriting 'Iolani Ranch someday?

Was he right?

Jonah wanted Darby to have the ranch, if she proved herself worthy of it. And he'd hinted—Darby smiled and sat a little straighter on her horse—that she was on the right track.

Was going back to Dee the only way Cade could ever be in charge of his own ranch?

If she had been sure of it, Darby would have told him things didn't have to be that way.

She tried not to daydream. Riding Hoku, she had to pay attention.

But Darby couldn't help picturing how it might be, ten or twelve years from now. She imagined Jonah, Aunty Cathy, and Ellen sitting on the lanai of Sun

House, looking down on the pasture where Megan and Cade were walking on each side of Biscuit, holding a little child centered in the buckskin's saddle.

She saw herself riding in from Pearl Pasture at a full gallop, dressed in jeans and a paniolo's hala hat; she'd be jumping a fence, and her long black braid and Hoku's golden tail would be streaking straight out behind them.

It was a good picture, a happy one. And it could happen if they all stuck together.

But where did that leave Dee?

Darby swallowed hard and felt a little guilty.

Dee was definitely not in Darby's picture.

Finally, just as the roof of Sun House showed above the trees, Darby thought of a conversational topic Cade shouldn't be touchy about.

"Did you hear we're herding the wild horses up toward Sky Mountain?" Darby asked.

"We?" Cade asked in a belittling tone.

Darby swallowed hard.

"I'm so happy to be an only child. I couldn't stand having a brother like you."

She managed to say it like a joke, but that single word vibrated between them until they reached home.

Okay, Darby thought as she brushed the dust from Hoku's coat. She knew she wasn't a good enough rider to go on the adventure.

Darby also knew why Cade had talked to her in

that tone, putting her down. He didn't want to talk. He wanted her to back off because his feelings were raw from his conversation with Dee.

Fine, but that was still no excuse for being mean.

But, Darby told herself later, Cade's unpleasantness did give her an excuse for not feeling like a traitor when she told Megan about Cade's encounter with Dee. And that's just what she did, while Megan chopped onions and Darby grated gingerroot for Aunty Cathy's tankatsu sauce that night.

"He's not seriously thinking of doing it? Moving back in with his mom, yeah?" Megan asked.

"I think he might be, but—ow!" Darby yelped as she grated a bit of her fingertip along with the ginger. She examined the scuff. "I'm not bleeding."

"Just like that?" Megan's voice sounded oddly nasal.

"Yeah, I was grating the ginger and—"

Megan sniffed, shook her head, and corrected Darby. "No, I mean Cade."

"Oh, well, he told her that before he'll move back, she has to do three things: divorce Manny, get a job, and stop smoking."

Megan was blinking back tears!

"I don't know Dee, but I don't think you have to worry." Darby tried to make Megan feel better. "I mean, I can't imagine her doing all those things. Not soon, anyway."

She looked over to see Megan use the back of

her wrist to wipe her eyes.

"Megan, don't cry," Darby begged.

"I'b not," Megan said, with a funny gulp. Then she fanned the air and explained, "The *onions*."

"Ohh," Darby said, relieved.

Finished with the task, Megan pushed aside the cutting board and went to the sink to wash her hands. "Actually, I'm happy."

Happy? That didn't make sense.

"So, uh, you don't think we have to worry?" Darby checked.

Megan turned back to the sink and shook the suds from her hands.

"Nope!" Megan definitely sounded smug.

"Why not?" Darby asked.

"Oh, nothing." Megan's singsong tone contradicted her words.

"What?" Darby demanded.

"It's just that, you know when I went down to talk to him? Well, I told him that if his mother wanted him to come home—"

"How did you know she would?"

"It just made sense. First there was Cade's dad, then Manny, and, I don't know, it just seems like she'd want him back, so I told him that I wouldn't blame him for going—"

"That was nice of you," Darby said sarcastically.

"Do you want to hear this?" Megan asked. "Because I'm good at giving advice, you know, but I don't throw my pearls before swine."

"Yes! I want to hear!"

"Okay." Megan gave a satisfied nod. "So, I said that if he didn't want to end up with things like they were before, he should have a list of demands, and he said, 'Like what?' And so we sat down together on the bunkhouse step and—"

"Those were *your* ideas?"

"No, they were totally his," Megan insisted. "I just put a little steel in his spine, yeah?"

 Chapter Eleven

The next morning was Friday, but Darby woke up to the smell of pancakes. They were usually a weekend treat, but since school was still closed, Jonah had made his special coconut pancakes. This was also surprising because Jonah hadn't eaten his tankatsu chicken dinner until eleven o'clock the night before.

Jonah, Kit, and Cade had stayed outside, working by porch light and flashlight to finish the cremellos' pasture fence. That meant they needed piping supplies from the hardware store in Hapuna for their next job.

Despite the aroma of pancakes, Jonah wasn't in the kitchen. But Megan was backing away from the refrigerator and Aunty Cathy was opening the oven.

"Good morning," Darby said.

"We're going into town." Megan shot her fist toward the ceiling in celebration.

"I have to arrange for more hay to be delivered—we didn't include the cremellos in our last order—and buy some replacement pipe for Flatlands." Aunty Cathy nodded toward one of the far pastures as she handed Darby pancakes on a warm plate. "If you girls can finish your chores and move the cremellos into their pasture by ten o'clock, you can come along to help me. If you want."

"Definitely," Darby agreed.

She shoveled down breakfast, pulled on boots and a sweatshirt, and got to work.

The dogs greeted them with barks of joy. Jack and Jill trotted at Darby's heels, waiting for her to do something more exciting than feed Francie the goat and her piglet, Pigolo. Knowing she'd spend even more time with Hoku, the Australian shepherds threw themselves down on their bellies. Muzzles between their front paws, they followed her with mournful brown eyes.

Darby glanced at the dogs while she hand-fed the sorrel wisps of hay.

This is so boring, the dogs' eyes seemed to say. But when it was time to lead the cremellos to their new pasture, the dogs knew it.

They sensed Darby's excitement as she went to meet Megan. The walk was short. It took fewer than five minutes to go from Hoku's pen to the gate, but the impatient neighs of the cremellos made Darby break into a jog.

Megan fell in beside her, and Bart streaked two circles around their legs before bouncing back to Cade.

Cade was working on something at the open gate. Perfectly balanced, he squatted at eye level with the bolt. His head was bent to his task, which involved rubbing something on the slide that extended into the fence post.

At first Darby thought it was a bar of soap. Then she caught the aroma of honey.

"Beeswax," Megan told her when she saw Darby lick her lips. "You wouldn't want to eat it, but it smells great, yeah?"

"Oh, yeah," Darby said as Cade stood and slipped the yellow-brown lump into his pocket.

"I've walked every inch of fence and made sure the bolt slides smoothly," Cade told them. He turned away to yawn, and Darby noticed a piece of blond hair straggling out from under his hat. Cade's tight paniolo braid was missing. It looked like he'd just stuffed his hair up under his hat.

"You were up late last night, weren't you?" Darby sympathized.

"What's your point?" Cade asked, then frowned at the gate as if she'd criticized his work.

As if on cue both girls held up their hands, pretending to ward off his crankiness, then headed for the round pen.

Cash, the first cremello Darby picked out, was well mannered enough not to drag Darby off her feet, but he pranced with excitement as she led him inside the gate of the grassy front pasture, slipped off his halter, and released him.

He scanned the enclosure, then burst into a run, tail cocked up high and streaming.

When the girls had moved all six of the cremellos, they leaned against the fence to watch them.

The pale horses raced over the grass, stopping to give bucks of joy, to roll with legs thrashing, then bolt to their hooves, to shake, and run again.

Although their coats ranged from stark white to tawny cream, all six horses had the same leggy conformation.

"Aren't they beautiful?" Megan asked.

"Like a flock of Pegasus, uh—"

"Pegasus*es*?" Megan suggested.

"Yeah," Darby said.

"Even though Babe takes good care of her horses, I bet this is the biggest pasture they've had for years," Megan mused.

Darby pictured her great-aunt Babe's Sugar Sands Cove Resort and nodded in agreement. The landscaped acres were designed to be a deluxe getaway for humans, not horses. The cremellos had lived in a well-tended paddock, but there hadn't been much room for stretching their long, slender legs.

All at once, Darby thought of Honi the pony, running on short, sturdy legs ahead of Hoku yesterday.

No matter what Dee wanted, someone should examine Honi.

Even if tests *were* expensive, and even if Dee was right that a vet couldn't "eyeball" the pony and make a diagnosis, someone had to take an interest in the elfin creature.

Elfin equine, Darby was thinking, when suddenly an idea popped into her mind.

Aunty Cathy had said they were going to the feed store. Cricket would be there. She'd talk to Cricket and see if the Animal Rescue Society had jurisdiction over animals that were allowed to run free. They might capture and keep the pony for her own good, just until the danger of disease had passed.

"Have fun!" Darby called to the cremellos, and then she tugged Megan's sleeve. "Let's go. We can't let your mom leave without us!"

The girls stampeded toward their rooms together, but Darby's face and hands were washed first and she was dressed in a clean yellow T-shirt, good jeans, and brown boots in under five minutes.

A record, Darby thought as she stood in front of Sun House. She'd taken her long hair out of its ponytail, brushed it briskly, and let it swing loose behind her back. She shifted restlessly, certain her blood was carbonated and fizzing in impatience.

Darby reminded herself that Honi had looked healthy, even perky, yesterday, but bacteria had a way of hiding inside for a while, didn't they? For Honi, every minute could count.

Megan and Aunty Cathy finally hurried down from their upstairs apartment, and they all climbed into the Land Rover.

"I wish you'd lose that hat," Aunty Cathy said. As she drove slowly out of the ranch yard, she glanced in the rearview mirror at the beloved baseball cap Megan wore, her ponytail poking through the back.

Megan's chin rose in stubbornness, but only for a few seconds. Then, she pulled off the cap, took down her hair, and fluffed it with her fingers.

"Hey, Mom?" Megan asked. "Do you know if Black Lava's herd is still on the football field?"

"They didn't move them yet, did they? They couldn't have!" Darby blurted, but Megan reached over and patted her hand in reassurance.

"I don't think so," Aunty Cathy said.

"Well, if they're still there, can we go see them?" Megan asked. "Before they're gone for good?"

"Maybe on the way home. Let's see how our time goes," Aunty Cathy replied.

They were only a few miles from 'Iolani Ranch when the signs of earthquake damage started to show.

"What are you so nervous about?" Megan asked Darby.

"I'm not," Darby said automatically.

"You're scratching your fingernails along the seams of your jeans," Megan observed.

"I'm worried about Honi, Cade's mom's pony."

"She's probably fine. If she's lived in Crimson Vale—or around there—for most of her life, she probably knows what to eat and drink, and I bet her immunities would be pretty good, right, Mom?"

"You'd have to ask a vet. Or Tutu." Aunty Cathy's voice piped higher at that idea. "I'm okay at patching up injuries, but when it comes to invisible bugs, I'm not much help."

"I'll talk to Cricket," Darby said, checking her plan with the others.

"Good idea," Megan said.

"It is. In fact, my first stop is the hardware store, but I can drop you at the feed store and come back," Aunty Cathy said, pulling into the parking lot at the rear of the feed store.

"Are you sure, Mom?" Megan asked.

"We have to help you load the pipe," Darby protested.

"I can get plenty of help at the hardware store. You two go ahead and talk horses with Cricket."

"I hope Cricket's working," Megan said as they climbed out of the car.

As they went through the back door, Darby breathed in the rich smells of grain and leather. Bags of feed—everything from chick scratch to broodmare chow—were piled to the ceiling, creating aisles.

They saw Cricket by stacks of baled hay. Her glasses had slid down her nose and she was peering over the tops of them, glancing between her clipboard and a tower of cardboard boxes.

She looked up at the sound of their steps and her businesslike smile broadened as she saw Megan and Darby coming toward her.

"Hey, girls!" she greeted them. "What's up?"

They'd just started to explain when the phone clipped to Cricket's belt rang. She held up one finger and answered it.

"Sorry," she said to the caller. "I know, and I'll be glad to write down your name, but—I know," she repeated, then glanced up at Megan and Darby and mouthed something that looked like *Tutu*.

Could that be right? Darby decided she must have misunderstood.

". . . last I heard she was back over Crimson Vale way. Good luck."

"Someone called here looking for Tutu? Really?" Darby asked as Cricket hung up the phone.

"It's been going on all week," Cricket said. "Almost everyone who's come in has seen Tutu or wants to get in touch with her."

As skilled as her great-grandmother was as an herbal healer, Darby was amazed. Tutu made her remedies and poultices in the kitchen of her small cottage, working amid bamboo wind chimes, jars of plants, shells, and herbs at an old-fashioned stove.

Her great-grandmother had no phone, no Internet or fax machine, and yet she managed to be there when people needed her.

"No one considers her age," Megan said, frowning.

"Not even her," Darby added, but she knew Megan was right.

Tutu was Jonah's mother and Jonah was in his fifties. Regardless of her good health, Tutu needed to catch a nap once in a while. Even her horse, Pretty-paint, was old.

"Have you talked to the men from the ARC today?" Megan asked.

Cricket shook her head, but her eyes strayed to Darby.

"I know," she said, still embarrassed. "Mr. Klaus and I didn't exactly hit it off."

Cricket chuckled. "You were pretty outspoken."

"I hate helicopter roundups, and it felt like he didn't even care if horses would get hurt. But, I—" Darby shook her head and swallowed hard. "I don't know what came over me."

"I do," Megan said. "You were the same way with Manny. You lose your temper when people hurt animals."

"*You* don't," Darby said, turning to Cricket.

"I'm not thirteen years old," Cricket whispered, and Darby laughed. From most other people, that would have sounded kind of uppity. But not from Cricket.

"There is that," Megan said, then turned toward the front of the store as she heard a woman's voice.

"Klaus isn't a horse guy," Cricket went on. "Or a people person for that matter, but he keeps an eye on government agencies, makes sure they stand behind farmers and ranchers. He's big on efficiency, and you were trying to derail his plan. I'm sure he didn't appreciate that."

"Especially not coming from a kid," Darby added. A *whiny* kid, she thought to herself, but Cricket just shrugged.

"Cute thing, though. Even though he's not a horse guy, he's getting kind of fond of Black Lava, yeah? He's over at the high school every minute he can get away. If we don't move the horses soon, he's ordering water trucked in. Would've done it already, but we're all out of troughs." Cricket gestured at the store and Darby nodded. 'Iolani wasn't the only ranch being cautious about water.

But Megan's mind had veered back to two mornings ago, when Darby and Ann had made their secret attempt to watch the wild horses.

"Awesome!" Megan cried. "The school gates will be unlocked if he's over there. And Mom said we could probably go. And this time"—Megan jabbed a gentle elbow in Darby's ribs—"you won't get detention."

"You girls want to help me unload this carton of fly spray?" Cricket asked.

They were almost finished putting the plastic spray bottles on a display, and Darby had just gotten the guts to ask Cricket about Honi, when the young woman said, "Since you girls aren't in school, we could use you as volunteers over at the rescue barn. The Department of Health is going to start quarantining horses they think might be sick and some will be kept there."

"Perfect," Darby said, but Cricket was moving among cardboard boxes, using a box cutter to slash them open, and didn't seem to hear.

"Taking precautions against salmonella—" Cricket glanced up to see their puzzlement. "Horses can develop it when they're under stress and these sure have been. So, we're scrubbing down every inch of every stall, every bucket, and every grain scoop. You name it and we're disinfecting it."

"As long as Jonah doesn't need us at the ranch, I'm in," Megan agreed.

"I'd like to do that," Darby said.

"Great," Cricket said. "I came into the store at seven this morning. I'll be off at three and go over to the barn. I'll work there until we're finished."

Cricket broke off to direct a customer to the bulletin board that listed livestock for sale and riding camps, and by the time she turned back to the girls, Darby had decided it would probably be better, and certainly more private, to talk with Cricket about Honi at the barn.

"We'll let you know," Megan promised.

"Just show up," Cricket said.

At that moment, Aunty Cathy came down the aisle and joined them.

"Did I see Cade's mom working at the front counter?" she asked Cricket.

"Yep. We put a 'help wanted' sign in the window yesterday, and I hired her this morning," Cricket confirmed.

Darby looked at Megan. Dee sure hadn't wasted any time in getting a job.

"What?" Cricket asked.

Darby knew Cricket had noticed their shocked expressions. Still, she said, "Nothing."

Telling Megan about Cade's deal with his mother was one thing, but Darby prided herself on not being a gossip. It would be wrong to tell Cade's business, or to prejudice Cricket against Dee.

Besides, Cricket knew all about Manny. She'd been there when he was arrested. Kit had even hinted that Cricket was the one who'd called Mr. Nomi and made sure he was there to slap handcuffs on Manny as soon as it was safe to drive down the hill that ended at his taro patch.

So, Cricket knew Dee's background.

Darby heard a slapping sound and saw Megan plucking at the blue plastic twine around a bale of hay.

Megan looked confused. She liked Cade. She didn't want to spread rumors about his mother, either. But just then, she gave the twine an extra hard twang, as if she'd made a decision.

"Did you notice if she was smoking?" Megan asked her mother, but it was Cricket who gasped.

"She'd better not be. We've got a warehouse full of hay and other flammable stuff." Cricket hustled off to the front of the store. "I'd better let her know that there's absolutely no smoking allowed. See you later, yeah?"

"Listen, girls," Aunty Cathy said. "If we're going to stop by school, let's get going. It's about to rain again." She nodded toward the front of the store. "I found a parking place on the street."

"Bye, Cricket," Darby said as the young woman walked back over to them.

Cricket made an "okay" sign with her fingers.

"Thanks for the heads-up on the cigarettes," she said quietly. Her eyes took in all three of them as she rewound her black hair and skewered it with a pencil. "And, Cathy, please tell them *yes* when they ask to work at the barn with me, yeah?"

They hurried up to the front door of the store.

Feeling guilty because Dee had to know they'd told Cricket about her smoking habit, Darby tried not to make eye contact with Dee at the cash register.

Darby thought she'd made it. Then, as she neared the door, Dee called to her—loudly.

Chapter Twelve

"Hey there, Miss Horse Charmer Junior!" Dee's voice sounded cheerful, and no one could have missed hearing it.

"I think that's for you," Megan said.

Darby's cheeks burned as two men looking at the silver-mounted headstalls turned to stare.

Since she couldn't ignore Cade's mother, Darby forced a smile before she even turned around. And she was glad she had.

Dee beamed proudly. She held out her arms as if she'd conquered this piece of Hawaii.

"Tell Cade to come see me at my new job!"

"I will," Darby promised.

"One down and two to go!" Dee crowed. Then

she punched a button on the cash register and when it beeped, she added, "Cha-ching!"

Megan must have told her mother the details of Cade's bargain with Dee, too, because even when they were back in the Land Rover, Aunty Cathy didn't ask what the woman was talking about.

With no pleading whatsoever, she drove toward Lehua High School, parked, and pulled a magazine out of the glove compartment.

"Thanks, Aunty Cathy," Darby said. "We won't be long."

"No more than twenty minutes," Aunty Cathy cautioned as they climbed out of the car.

"Yes, Mom." Megan drew out the words to sound long-suffering and pitiful.

"And girls?" Aunty Cathy inquired with such scary slowness, they both froze. "When you get back, we'll be having a talk about why Darby is on detention."

They ran most of the way to the football field only to see the wild herd had been moved to the *baseball* field.

The Cyclone fences formed a corral for Black Lava's herd, but they must be grazing behind the bleachers, because Darby didn't see them.

The humid air crowded into her lungs, and she slowed to a jog when she saw Mr. Klaus standing at the gate with his arms crossed. He made a megaphone of his hands and shouted, "Sorry, girls! No one's allowed near the wild horses."

Megan rolled her eyes and slowed to a walk.

"He likes Black Lava," Darby reminded them both.

"He's just not a people person." Megan tried to sound sympathetic, but when she repeated Cricket's assessment of Mr. Klaus, she couldn't contain a giggle.

Darby walked with her hands on her hips, still trying to catch her breath.

"What do you think the chances are that he'll let me go on the horse drive, if I'm nice to him?"

"Zero," Megan said, "and even if he does, Kit won't, and even if Kit does, Jonah won't, and—"

By then, Darby had a deep-enough breath for a loud sigh.

"Sorry, sis," Megan told Darby as she hugged her shoulders, "but my mom's already passed out a bunch of rules about me going."

Darby's hands slipped off her hips. She surrendered to reality, but she didn't like it.

"I can't ride Tango, for instance," Megan said. "She wants me to ride Navigator, since, you know."

Which meant that even if Jonah lost his mind and forgot his promises to her mother, Aunty Cathy would take a stand to keep her from going.

"So, if it's hopeless, why should I be nice to him?" Darby grumbled when they'd nearly reached Mr. Klaus.

"Because you're a lovely young lady?" Megan widened her eyes dramatically, and Darby was about to give her a shove when she noticed Mr. Klaus was very nearly *smiling* at them.

Until he realized who they were.

"I should've guessed," he said.

"Hi, Mr. Klaus," Megan said.

"Hi," Darby echoed.

If she was going to apologize for yesterday's behavior, now was the time. But what if he got the wrong idea about the helicopters? She'd back down from being a brat but not from protecting the horses.

He was already watching her suspiciously.

"Cricket told us you were keeping watch over the horses," Darby said, "and we wanted to see if we could help out."

He must have realized it was true, because he uncrossed his arms, opened the gate, and let them join him inside the fenced field.

"They're over behind the bleachers, taking shelter from that wind," he said.

The wind wasn't cold, but it smelled stormy, Darby thought. Along with Mr. Klaus and Megan, she glanced up at a sky that had turned from morning's bright blue to the sullen color of a bruise.

"More rain's coming," Mr. Klaus observed. "And the horses need it, but the troughs I ordered from Honolulu aren't here yet, and we'll be moving the horses out tomorrow." He looked at Darby. When she stayed still and silent, he went on, "Until then, we've just got those plastic buckets and they're drinking from water in the low places—over there by home plate, especially," he said, pointing. "I wish the school—"

"Oh! I've got it!" Megan yelled. "Ever since Cricket mentioned they were out of troughs, I've been seeing this weird picture in my head, but now I know what it is! The bathtubs. They'll be perfect!"

"Excuse me?" Mr. Klaus looked confused.

"Last year our school had bathtub races in the ocean. Each class had a team—you know, the freshmen, the sophomores—and we all had to make our own tubs," Megan said.

"How do you do that?" Darby asked.

"They weren't real bathtubs," Megan explained. "More like little boats that *looked* like bathtubs, but they had to be able to float and hold a crew of at least four. Every year local companies compete down at Hapuna harbor, but this was our school version of it."

"And they're kept—?"

"In the old ball shed," Megan said. "The new shed, where we keep soccer balls and cones and stuff like that, is locked, but the old one isn't."

The colorful tub boats were unwieldy, but not too heavy, and they got them out just as it began to rain.

"The horses probably wouldn't come near this one," Megan said, yanking at a tub painted with colorful scales. A plywood dragon's head was attached to the front.

As soon as it was fully out of the shed, a commanding neigh blasted from behind the bleachers.

Neck arched, the black stallion emerged snorting, ready for battle.

"I don't think he likes the look of it," Darby said. "Should we leave it inside the shed?"

"I guess," Megan said.

Even as they pushed it back inside the shed, Black Lava stood watch.

Soon the field boasted four tubs collecting rain-water.

Darby heard Aunty Cathy honk the Land Rover's horn.

"We've got to go," Megan apologized.

"This is wonderful," Mr. Klaus said, rain dripping off his nose as he walked the girls back to the gate. "Thank you, ladies, so much. Would you like to come into the school and dry off?"

"No thanks," Megan declined. "My mom's waiting for us."

"Well, thank you once again," Mr. Klaus said.

Darby found herself waiting for him to say something like "I'm sorry for having misjudged you," or "You are the two most capable young people I've ever met," but it didn't happen.

While Darby was waiting for Megan to climb into the Land Rover ahead of her, she glanced back at the field.

Black Lava strode around the old ball shed, stopping every few steps to sniff for trouble.

A guy can't be too careful, Darby thought, and the stallion's vigilance made her feel a little better about his upcoming move to Sky Mountain.

"Sorry to interrupt your good deed," Aunty Cathy said as they fastened their seat belts for the trip home. She gestured with her cell phone. "Jonah called, and Kimo came back to work before he should have, and he says Tutu's coming to the ranch, but he'd like me to see what I can do for Kimo in the meantime. It doesn't sound like an emergency, but I guess Kimo refuses to stay in the bunkhouse to rest, so we get to be his jailers."

As soon as they pulled up in front of Sun House, they saw a familiar, sturdily built figure walking toward them from the direction of the bunkhouse.

"Jonah was right." Aunty Cathy shook her head as she parked the car and pulled on the emergency brake.

"Kimo!" Darby cried, nearly jumping out of the car. "How are you feeling?"

"Better," Kimo said, but there was a wash of paleness over his tanned face and his eyes looked tired. "I'm on my way out to Pearl Pasture, but I just needed to sit a minute."

There was no horse saddled and waiting for him by the tack shed, but Darby didn't offer to catch one. Kimo didn't look healthy enough to be out of bed, let alone riding and working in the rain.

"Tutu was at my place," Kimo said, "and I tried to

give her a lift over here, but someone told her about some sick horse, and she's out looking for it on Pretty-paint. Lady doesn't know when to slow down."

Megan cleared her throat loudly.

"You don't be givin' me the stink eye, Mekana. I'm good to ride. Biscuit is tied over on the other side of the bunkhouse, waiting for me."

"Okay." Megan sounded dubious, and when Kimo turned too quickly and put his hand to his head as if the movement had made him dizzy, Aunty Cathy reached for his arm.

"Cathy, now you get back." Kimo waved her off. Then he headed toward the tack shed.

"That's one stubborn cowboy," Megan drawled.

"Ridiculous," Aunty Cathy said to the girls. "I'm going to ride with him. I'm sure there'll be something for me to do and at least if he falls off, I'll be there to catch Biscuit."

"Want us to do something while you're gone, Mom?"

"Stay here," Aunty Cathy said. "With all that plastic pipe, I didn't have room for the hay, so the feed store's delivering it. The driver will have an invoice marked 'paid,' and all you have to do is count how much hay I paid for and how much they leave. They'll match, and then you just sign for it."

"It's not as complicated as it sounds," Megan told Darby as her mother left. "I've done it lots of times."

While the girls waited, they played with Blue Moon

once the rain stopped. The foal looked happy and healthy and he'd learned to trade snorts with Hoku, even though their corrals were some distance apart.

Fun made the time go fast. It wasn't long before they heard a motor. A big flatbed truck piled with hay was rumbling up the road.

Shading her eyes, Megan studied it.

"Can you believe it?" she asked.

Darby followed Megan's stare. Sun glazed the truck's windshield, but she could see through it clearly enough to identify the driver.

"Dee's delivering hay," Darby said.

A minute later, with a noisy grinding of gears, the truck jerked to a stop.

"Hey there, girls," Dee said as she vaulted to the ground. "Got some hay here for you. Where's that son of mine? Tell him to come and help us unload it."

Darby and Megan exchanged glances. They couldn't blame Dee for wanting Cade to see her working, but they hadn't even had a chance to tell him she'd been hired yet.

"He's up in Flatlands pasture," Darby told her. "We'll help you unload."

Dee's face drooped in disappointment, but when Peach, the sweetest of the Australian shepherds, came up and nuzzled her hand, Dee shrugged.

"Oh well, then," she said, then climbed onto the truck bed and began tossing bushels of hay down to Megan and Darby.

Darby didn't know why she'd thought Dee was soft. Cade's mother moved with quick strength that made Darby believe the woman really had helped Manny work his taro patch.

In fact, Darby and Megan worked hard to stack the hay as fast as Dee threw it down, and Darby had the feeling Dee had done most of the labor on their hardscrabble farm.

At last Dee stopped. She dusted her hands together and climbed back down to the ground. She leaned into the truck cab and withdrew some papers.

"Which of you wants to sign this invoice?" Dee asked.

"You can," Megan said, so Darby took the papers.

Remembering what Aunty Cathy had told her, Darby quickly counted up the number of bales they'd stacked while Dee threw a stick for Peach.

"There's a mistake," Darby said to Megan. They did a second count, then Darby called to Dee, "We've got four bales too many."

"Well, look at you, all checking the invoice and like that," Dee said, but she didn't seem surprised.

Darby grabbed the twine around one bale. "It's okay. We'll just throw them back on the truck."

Dee held up her hand to stop Darby. "Don't bother. The feed store has lots more where that came from. They won't miss it. Tell Cade it's a gift from me."

"No, really," Megan protested. "Take it back. My mom wouldn't want it if we didn't pay for it."

"But it's a gift. You know what they say about looking a gift horse in the mouth."

"Actually, I don't," Megan said.

"They say don't do it," Dee snapped. She got back into the truck cab. "Tell Cade I'm staying with my friend Lisa Miller in town if he needs me. Manny's truck broke down, and I'd have no way to get to my new job if I stayed out in Crimson Vale. Be sure to tell him because I know how worried he got last time he couldn't find me."

"Who's taking care of Honi?" Darby asked.

"My smart little pony takes care of herself," Dee said. The engine roared to life, but then Dee shouted out the window. "Come to think of it, since you don't want it, maybe Cade can drop one of these bales of hay over there for Honi."

Darby opened her mouth to speak but no words came out.

Dee had been on the job less than a day and she was already stealing from the feed store. She called it a gift, but Darby wasn't so sure Dee hadn't thought of the gift as pony food on her way over here.

Waving, Dee revved the truck engine. Then, she backed up so fast, Darby covered her eyes.

"Don't hit the fence. Don't hit the fence. Please don't hit the fence," Megan chanted.

When a full minute passed without the sound of a crash, Darby peeled her fingers away from her eyelids. Dust rolled up from the flatbed's back tires, and it was going too fast, but Dee had missed the new pasture fence.

"Did we just receive stolen goods?" Megan asked.

Darby stood staring after the truck. It made a left on the highway and drove out of sight. "I'm not quite sure what happened."

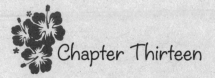

Chapter Thirteen

That evening after the dinner dishes had been cleared, everyone assembled on the Sun House lanai to discuss driving the horses up to the mountains the next day. While Kit, Aunty Cathy, Kimo, Megan, and Cade sat talking, Darby kept silent.

She'd phoned Patrick just before dinner, and they'd conspired to have Patrick's mother drive them to the school tomorrow at dawn. Together, they'd get to the top of the bleachers with binoculars, and at least that way they could see the wild horses leave, even if they couldn't go along.

Darby sighed, then caught Jonah's wink. He motioned for her to follow him inside the house.

"You know why you're not riding along, Darby Leilani, yeah?"

"I'm too inexperienced. I get that, but right after the tsunami I helped drive the wild horses from the *kipuka* to the high school," she reminded him.

"You did good that day," he said, "but this will be a tougher drive."

"I know," she said, and though it took some effort to keep the whine out of her tone, Darby knew in her heart that he was right.

The riders would have their hands full. They'd have to be alert for drop-offs, holes rooted by feral pigs, and the sudden appearance of anything that could spook the horses. If she got into a situation she couldn't handle, she'd ruin everything.

But logic didn't make Darby feel any better. She felt let down and a little embarrassed to be singled out as the only one on the ranch who wasn't up to the challenge.

Her feelings must have shown on her face. "Hey, there will be other things like this for you to go on, yeah?" Jonah said in a voice that was—for him—unusually gentle. "It's just that you haven't been riding long enough. That's all."

"I understand," Darby said.

Jonah put his hand on her shoulder and squeezed lightly. "We'll need you and Kimo here to look after the ranch."

She knew he was giving her his vote of confidence, telling her she had to stay behind, so that she couldn't even go stand in the bleachers with Patrick and—

"Me and *Kimo*?" Darby asked.

Jonah nodded and Darby winced. If she felt put

down and abandoned, Kimo must feel a hundred times worse.

"Your tutu's overdoing it." Jonah looked angry instead of worried. "I want someone here who can drive her to—" He made a vague gesture. "She's a madwoman, but if she suddenly comes into some good sense and gives that poor old paint horse a rest, Kimo can drive her on her rounds."

Darby stepped out the front door of Sun House and inhaled the warm, moist air.

Longing wrapped around her and she suddenly missed her mother, even though it hadn't been very long since Ellen was at the ranch.

Since Ellen was across the ocean in Tahiti, Darby walked toward Hoku's corral. She and the wild filly had a heart-to-heart communication that was as good, or better, than speech.

When the filly saw Darby, she came to her right away, shaking her head and snorting in greeting. Even in the dusky glow of the day's last light Hoku's sleek skin gave off copper glints.

Sliding the bolt on Hoku's gate, Darby stepped inside. "Hey, pretty girl. Are you okay?"

"Blue Moon just has colic," she reassured her horse, but Darby was thinking that in epidemics the young and old went first. She thought of Judge and Pretty-paint and tried to shake the image from her head.

Selfishly, she was glad Cade hadn't agreed to

bring Honi up to 'Iolani Ranch. She ran her hand along Hoku's side and took in the mustang's smooth warmth.

"I couldn't stand it if anything happened to you," she said softly.

Hoku stared at her.

"Aren't we communicating tonight?" she asked her horse.

Hoku pawed at the ground, then nudged Darby nearly off her feet.

Too much drama, the filly seemed to say, and then she swished her tail and walked to the other side of the corral.

Laughing, Darby started walking back up to Sun House. Hoku always knew what she needed, and this time it had been a signal to get a grip. Her life was practically perfect, and she and Hoku would have plenty of rides together.

Darby's steps slowed as she realized that in all the excitement about driving the horses to Sky Mountain, she and Megan hadn't found time to tell anyone about the extra bales of hay Dee had left behind as *gifts.*

She wondered if she should say anything. It was stealing and Cricket should know about it. But she was nervous about being the one to tell.

Through the dim light Darby saw Jonah approaching.

Should she tell him what Dee had done? Jonah erased her impulse in a hurry.

"I'm done arguing. If Kimo shows up at the school tomorrow planning to drive horses, he's fired."

The next morning, everyone was up before dawn for the horse drive. Yawning, Darby pulled herself out of bed, slipped on her robe, and came out of her room.

Megan was already standing in the hall dressed in chaps and a denim shirt. "I told Cade about Dee's job," she reported to Darby.

"What did he say?"

"He said, 'Good for her.' He seemed happy."

"Did you say anything about the . . . hay?"

Megan shook her head. "Do you think I should?"

"Not yet. I'll figure something out today."

"Okay. Have you seen my heavy riding gloves?" Megan asked. "The black ones?"

"I think you stuck them inside your boots at the door the last time you rode Tango. Remember?" Darby recalled.

"That's right. Thanks," Megan said and was off to get them.

Darby heard a brief clatter of dishes from the kitchen and the sound of animated voices. The door opened and closed a few times, and then there was quiet.

Outside, every truck left towing a horse trailer. Every truck except Kimo's, Darby corrected herself.

The night before, Jonah had bullied Kimo into staying in the bunkhouse overnight, so he could help out Darby during the day.

As she walked around the empty house, she decided he wasn't up yet.

After a brief volley of barking, the dogs were quiet and the ranch yard seemed just as deserted as the house.

Darby dressed, ate a quick bowl of cereal, and went outside to free the five big dogs from their kennel and feed the animals.

Twice, she thought she heard the phone ringing, and the third time she sprinted back to the kitchen to double-check.

She wasn't hearing things. Darby rushed to pull off her boots and answer it. She had time, because whoever was calling had decided to let it ring until she finally answered.

"Hello?" Darby gasped.

"Darby Leilani!" Tutu shouted.

"Are you all right?" Darby asked. Thank goodness Jonah had insisted Kimo stay behind.

"Can you hear me?" Tutu's voice was so loud, it was as if she didn't trust the phone lines to do the job of carrying her voice. That made sense, Darby figured, since Tutu didn't even have a phone.

"Darby!"

"Yes, I can hear you." Darby held the receiver away from her ear a little.

"Get someone with a horse trailer. Have them meet me at Dee's pond."

Oh, no. Jonah had said Tutu was searching for a

sick horse. It had to be Honi.

"Dee's pond! Did you hear?"

"I heard," Darby said. "Dee's pond, with a horse trailer. But Tutu—"

Her great-grandmother hung up before Darby could tell her that every horse trailer on the ranch was gone.

Darby ran toward the bunkhouse. Kimo met her halfway.

"Aloha," he greeted her. "When I took Blue Moon and Blue Ginger back to their pasture, I brought up Baxter for me and Lady Wong for you."

It took Darby a few seconds to realize Navigator, Kona, Biscuit, and many of the other horses were gone. But it didn't really matter, since the next thing she'd be riding, if she was lucky, would be a truck.

Darby gave Kimo a quick once-over. His color was normal and his eyes were no longer dull.

"You look better," Darby said, but she was thinking, *Healthy enough to drive, at least.* "And it's a good thing. Tutu just called and said to meet her at Dee's pond with a horse trailer. She has a really sick horse that she wants to bring here—"

"All trailers're gone?" Kimo asked, scanning the ranch yard.

"Yes, but . . ." Darby paused as her brain spun. Then she stared at Kimo's battered burgundy Ram Charger. Wishing she was better at math so she could estimate the square footage of its cargo space, she went on hesitantly, "I'm almost positive it's Honi, Dee's pony. I think she might fit in the back of your truck."

"Mo' bettah we try than give up," Kimo said. Then, without explaining what he was doing, he ran back into the bunkhouse and reemerged with an armload of black plastic garbage bags and pointed to the back of his truck.

They didn't exactly organize all the CDs, newspapers, and food wrappers that they found in the back of Kimo's truck. Instead, they just shoved everything into the bags and then Darby jumped up into the back with a broom while Kimo ran to get some tattered blankets from the bunkhouse.

"That'll have to do 'er," he said, and then they piled into the truck.

It had been twenty minutes since Tutu had called.

As they drove, the radio blared, and they heard a news story about pockets of salmonella being found all over the island among animals and humans. Darby was pretty sure the reporter said that the condition could be contagious between humans and animals, but it was hard to tell because every time Kimo hit a bump, his radio lost the signal for a few seconds.

Kimo was about to turn toward Crimson Vale, and Darby was remembering the sickening drive that he'd taken her on on the day of her arrival, when a Jeep that looked like it had barely survived a garage fire barreled halfway through the intersection and stopped right in front of them.

With luck, Kimo wouldn't hit it broadside.

 Chapter Fourteen

There were just the two vehicles—Kimo's and the Jeep—so when the Jeep began honking and flashing its lights, Kimo and Darby looked at each other.

Kimo raised his hand to give the crazy driver a cautious shaka just as Darby recognized Cricket. But what was Cricket doing here? Why wasn't she helping to drive Black Lava's herd to Sky Mountain?

Cricket drove toward them and pulled up next to the driver's-side window.

"We have to quarantine them in a separate corral. They're really afraid it'll spread like wildfire across the island." She broke off, seeing their confusion. "You *are* coming to volunteer, yeah?" she asked hopefully, but she didn't give Darby a chance to answer. "Ann's already there and we could·really use your help. The Department of Ag is sending us more sick animals than we can handle. It's insane here. That's why I stayed behind."

Darby's mother might not want her among the sick horses. Neither would Jonah. And Hoku—

"Go," Kimo urged Darby. "I'll pick you up once I have Tutu and the pony."

"Okay," Darby said.

She opened the door and jumped out of the truck. For a minute she thought she might have to chase after Cricket, but she hopped into the ugly Jeep just in time.

Once inside, Darby tightened her seat belt a little snugger than usual. This morning Cricket's messy bun was stabbed into place by a red lacquered chopstick, and she was talking to herself as she drove.

They almost passed the Animal Rescue barn, and Cricket cranked the steering wheel so hard to the right, the Jeep tilted up on two wheels.

"I don't usually drive like this," Cricket apologized, and then, while Darby was catching her breath, Cricket said, "We're here."

The place was a madhouse.

Behind the barn there was a field where most of the horses were kept.

All around, volunteers and vets worked in teams to tend to the sick horses.

"Darby!" Ann's curly red hair was like a beacon

amid all the people who'd gathered to help. She bolted out of the crowd and hugged Darby. "I'm going crazy from boredom and I've missed your face!" She pressed her cheek to Darby's.

Then they both looked for Cricket. They spotted her watching a woman who was mopping down a feverish mare. A few yards away, five young men threw their weight into the side of a bay gelding, trying to keep him from lying down.

"What should we do?" Ann asked, but at the same time several other people saw Cricket, recognized her as the boss of the frantic situation, and began shouting questions at her.

A gray-haired man extended a bucket handle toward Darby.

"Could you fill this with water?" he asked.

"No, she can't!" Cricket said, blocking Darby's reach. "I want you two to stay in the office answering phones. There are maps taped to the desks. Give volunteers who call directions on how to get here. And if they just want to drop off money, take it. Hey, Lisa! Lisa Miller!"

Cricket waved to get a woman's attention. The name was familiar, but Darby didn't recognize her.

"You've got a litter of pups at home, don't you, Lisa? That's what I thought. Get away from that colt. You don't want to make your own babies sick."

"But we know what we're doing with horses," Ann protested when Cricket finally looked back at the girls.

"That's just the point," Cricket insisted. "I don't want anyone who's going to have contact with horses in the next forty-eight hours going into that barn. Be right back."

Cricket took the bucket herself and dashed toward a silver tanker at the far end of the field. She stood in a line of volunteers, all waiting for water.

Beyond Cricket, Darby saw a pewter-gray horse flecked with black. It looked like Medusa, the wild mustang Kit had adopted. As Darby tried to get a better look at the horse, a man shouting into a cell phone about medicinal suppositories jostled her, and she lost sight of the horse.

"Let's go inside," Darby said, grabbing Ann's arm. "It's making me crazy that I can't help."

For the next hour, she, Ann, and the thirtyish woman named Lisa managed the phones as Cricket had asked them to do.

Cricket stuck her head in once to say that they were supposed to discourage people from bringing more animals to the center.

"Right now, I'm praying that the plane that's supposed to pick up all the non-equines is really going to land at Hapuna Airport and take these poor critters to the Humane Society on Oahu. They have much better facilities—" Cricket was gone before she finished the sentence.

Between phone calls, Darby, Ann, and Lisa had choppy conversations.

"It's so good to see somebody besides Toby and Buck," Ann said, referring to her younger brothers.

"Kimo and Tutu are picking up the pony and as soon as he shows up, I've got to go with them—"

"—house guest *and* a litter of pit bull pups, but she'll be gone when I get home because—"

"—have no idea what it's like playing dress-up and magic show instead of—"

"And I want to be generous, but I'm afraid for Hoku—"

"—lowlife *snitch* ratted her out for making a first-day mistake and she lost the only decent job she's ever had!"

Darby's stomach dropped sickeningly. Now she knew why Lisa Miller's name sounded familiar. Dee had said she was staying in town with her girlfriend Lisa Miller and leaving Honi to fend for herself.

But Darby hadn't told anyone about the stolen hay. What had Dee done to get fired?

"Aren't you just amazed at the number of people who are calling to help?" Ann asked.

"All the phones have stopped ringing, but not my ears," Lisa Miller said.

Darby glanced at the clock. Kimo and Tutu would have to be back soon, wouldn't they? It was lunchtime. She'd been here for two hours.

"How's everything going in here?" Cricket came in and surveyed the office.

"Fine, but Cricket"—Darby stood, keeping her

back to Lisa Miller as she lowered her voice—"I have to tell you, four extra bales of hay were accidentally delivered to the ranch."

Cricket rolled her eyes. "We had lots of those *accidents* yesterday, and the 'help wanted' sign is back in the window."

Darby didn't have any idea how much a bale of hay was worth, but she reached in her pocket.

"I have some money," she said.

"Don't touch me!" Cricket yelped. "I shouldn't even be around you guys. Darby, you could infect Hoku."

With her head, she motioned for Darby to step outside the office.

"I know Jonah's good for a few dollars' worth of hay," she said. "Keep your money in your pocket. But thanks for being honest."

Just then Kimo's Ram Charger pulled up to the curb.

Tutu's white hair shone from the passenger's seat. She was half turned around, looking back at Honi.

"Is that a horse in the back of Kimo's truck?" Cricket asked. "Oh, no you don't." She ran around to the driver's window. "You can't leave her here, Kimo. No! I'm sorry, but there's no room for her. I just can't!"

For the first time during this crazy day, it sounded to Darby as if Cricket was losing her grip on her emotions.

Tutu's melodious voice soothed over all the other sounds, and though Darby couldn't tell what her great-grandmother said, Cricket's shoulders sagged in relief.

Tutu opened her door and beckoned for Darby to climb in, but she held a finger against her lips.

Every time she saw Tutu, it was like seeing a glimpse of her future, Darby thought. In her pink shawl and loose-fitting purple dress, Tutu had the strong posture of a young woman, but white hair fell in wisps from the scarf tied around her oval face.

Heavy dark brows topped piercing eyes. And if they'd been blue like Darby's, instead of brown, Tutu could have been Darby in about seventy more years.

Darby crept into the truck as quietly as she could, but the front seat was open to the truck bed and she still wakened the pony.

Honi lay on her side in the back of the truck. As they drove away from the Animal Rescue barn, she began rolling.

"Tutu," Darby said, "Honi's really sick, isn't she?"

"As soon as we can get her on her feet and walking, we'll see."

Tutu opened her medicine bag and took out a twist of waxed paper.

"I need to put this into the corner of her mouth," she told Darby.

"What is it?"

Tutu poured something that looked like pizza seasoning onto her palm. "A mix of herbs to keep her calm until we can get her out of here," Tutu said, and then, with surprising flexibility for a woman her age, she hung over the seat. Kimo drove smoothly as she petted the pony's coarse mane and talked to her in Hawaiian.

Darby didn't offer to help. It didn't seem right to make Tutu do this alone, but she had Hoku and the other 'Iolani horses to consider.

For a single instant, the pony's eyelids snapped open and the whites were all Darby could see of her eyes. Honi moved her lips in rubbery attempts to escape Tutu's index finger as she slipped the herbs into the corner of her mouth. And then the pony sighed, as if she was too weary to fight the indignity.

"I think you got them all into her mouth," Darby said.

Tutu settled back into her seat and pulled her pink shawl closer around her shoulders. She looked like she could use a nap, Darby thought, but her great-grandmother was wide-awake and thinking.

"Where should we put her when we get back to the ranch?" Tutu asked Kimo.

"Hmph?" Kimo jerked as if the question had startled him.

Or maybe Tutu had wakened him. Since he was the one driving, that was a scary thought.

"Round pen," he recommended, and Darby nodded.

That was the best suggestion, but what if Honi's illness was contagious? Could it become airborne and infect the other horses?

Thank goodness Blue Moon had recovered from

his colic and Kimo had moved him this morning. The broodmares, foals, and yearlings in the lower pasture would be safe, but what about Hoku and the cremellos?

She hoped Jonah, Kit, or Aunty Cathy would be home when they got there. But she knew it was unlikely. They'd planned to be gone until sundown.

Darby's heart beat like a metronome. It was up to her. She was in charge of the horses while Jonah was away. She had to keep them safe.

Seven horses. Hoku and the cremellos depended on her.

Wait, she had to add two more, because Kimo had left Buckin' Baxter and Lady Wong tied by their neck ropes, waiting patiently for them to return.

Nine horses. Could she risk leaving them close to the infected pony? Could she refuse to turn Hoku loose because she was afraid she'd run wild in the pastures below Sun House?

How could she know her choices were the right ones?

"Tutu, how did you know the water was contaminated?" Darby felt guilty for not noticing anything except the dead mongoose—and taking so long to worry about that!

"It wasn't difficult for a practiced eye," Tutu said. "There was wilting plant life, very few insects, and the water lilies were completely gone."

"Oh, it wasn't like that when Cade and I were up there."

Darby shuddered. The pond had been nearly covered in the flowers. Tutu described how she'd dropped to her knees beside the pond and used a stick to probe it. All the water lilies had died and turned into mushy brown sludge on the pond bottom.

"And then I heard thrashing in the bushes and found this poor little one," Tutu said. "I recognized her and went to Dee's house. Even though no one was home, I used that phone. And then you came to our rescue."

"What about Prettypaint?" Darby asked.

"I left her there. She deserves a rest."

"So do you," Darby said. She tried not to notice the ashy circles under Tutu's eyes as she kissed her great-grandmother's cheek.

"I'll sleep when I am old," Tutu joked. "Right now I have work to do. Once we've got Honi moving, I'll go up to Sun House and make a poultice of chamomile, lavender, and tea tree oil for his head."

"Whose head?" Kimo asked.

"Yours, stubborn boy," Tutu snapped. "It will stop the throbbing and lower your fever. And please don't tell me you're just fine."

"I *am* fine," Kimo insisted as he turned down the dirt road to 'Iolani Ranch. "For a sick guy who lifted a horse."

The dogs ran out barking to greet them, and Kimo drove as close to the round pen as he could get before he asked, "And now I suppose you want me to do it again?"

"If you please," Tutu said graciously, and Kimo groaned.

* * *

By the time Kimo braked to a stop, Darby had made up her mind, and Honi was no longer thrashing.

Darby didn't know if that was a good thing or not. She didn't touch Honi, but she bent close to the pony's pink nostrils to check her respiration. Honi was breathing faster than Hoku did, but maybe that was because she was a smaller animal.

"Kimo," Darby said as they stood at the back of his truck. "Are you up to a horse drive of our own?"

"Depends," he said.

Darby didn't let his fatigue stop her from laying out her idea. There was too much at stake to be softhearted.

"Once we get Honi inside the round pen, I want to take Hoku and the cremellos down to the lower pastures. We'll ride Baxter and Lady Wong down and leave them, too—"

"He must shower and change clothes first," Tutu instructed. "In case the pony's contagious."

Darby nodded and went on. "—and walk back. That way, Honi will sort of be in quarantine." She looked at him with pleading eyes, but she wasn't begging for approval like a little kid. "Okay? Are there any holes in that plan?"

"Probably," Kimo said. "But it's the best plan we've got, so let's saddle up, *keiki*."

Chapter Fifteen

"It's not a trap, baby."

Darby had opened Hoku's gate from Lady Wong's saddle, and the sorrel filly wouldn't come near the opening in her fence. She trotted a graceful, floating circle around her corral, flashing her ears in all directions, but she'd smelled the new pony, and she was suspicious.

Freshly showered, Kimo flung open the cremellos' gate. Whooping and spinning his arm on high, as if he held a rope, he urged the high-spirited white horses out of the pasture they'd just learned to call home.

Taking her cue from Kimo, Darby rode close enough to grab the tangerine-and-white lead rope off Hoku's corral fence.

She spun it over her head, even though Hoku shied in fear and ducked.

"There they go!" Darby yelled.

Hoku bolted, but not for the gate.

The rope was too close to her escape route, so the filly sprinted, gathered herself for the very short lead up to the jump, and cleared her corral fence.

Please don't let her remember she just did that, Darby begged silently.

Animals live in the moment, Jonah had told her once, so Darby decided to make sure Hoku wouldn't remember, by not giving her time to look back and think about it.

"Run, girl!" She rode Lady Wong as fast as she could after Hoku, and the filly broke into a gait faster than a gallop. She swept past the sixth cremello, then the fifth, and finally, belly almost touching the ground, she dashed through the center of the pale herd and left them and Kimo behind.

Hoku knew where she was headed, down to the pasture below, and she knew Darby was the one who'd forced her to go.

"I'm gonna rest up a little," Kimo said.

They'd climbed back up the trail to Sun House carrying the saddles and bridles they'd stripped off their mounts, and Kimo's steps were weaving with weariness.

As he meandered toward the bunkhouse, Darby

hung up their gear and walked back to the round pen to watch Tutu and the pony.

"She's a little bit interested in her surroundings. That's good," Tutu said.

Although Honi was still down, the pony was on her knees, not her back or side, and Tutu sat next to her. When Tutu gently rolled back Honi's eyelid, the pony didn't protest. Instead, she reached up her nose as if they were sharing a secret.

Darby smiled. Honi was living up to her name— Kiss—and she was kissing Tutu.

"Should you let her do that? Aren't you afraid you'll get sick?" Darby asked.

"I've already been exposed to everything this island can throw at me this week," Tutu said. "If this helps her feel better, it's worth it. I want her up on all four hooves, but she won't open her eyes." Tutu mused, "Perhaps she hasn't been able to sleep for some time, because of the pain. We'll let her have a nap and then try again."

When her great-grandmother came out of the corral, they still watched Honi, and Darby told Tutu about the sick animals at the Animal Rescue Society barn and about Dee stealing the hay.

"And it wasn't like she was trying to get something for nothing," Darby said slowly. "She wanted to show off for Cade and she was so disappointed he wasn't here. He never made it into the feed store to see her at the cash register, either, and she was kind of proud."

Tutu shook her head sadly. "I've known Dee since she was a little girl. She always wanted to be somebody important. She had big dreams of being a nurse." Tutu smiled. "But then she married and had Cade and she quit school. She began caring for a child when she was still a child herself. She stopped developing as a person. She's still like a sixteen-year-old inside or like one of those water lilies Honi is always munching."

"What do you mean?" Darby asked.

"When tropical water lilies are planted too early they never grow as well as they should."

Leaving Darby to mull that over, Tutu told Darby to stay with Honi while she went up to Sun House.

"I'm not sure what to watch for," Darby said.

"Don't worry. She's got the medicine inside," Tutu answered, "but we have to get her up and moving so it can travel through her gut and do some real good.

"I'll go up to the kitchen and make that poultice for Kimo. Try not to disturb her." Tutu glanced up at the sun as if reading a clock. "Let's give her thirty minutes of uninterrupted rest. Then, when I get back, if I can't get her up, we'll bring the goat over and see if she can get Honi moving."

Tutu had been gone for only a few minutes when Darby heard a car slow down, a door open and close, and then, as the car sped away, shoes cross the steel cattle guard set at the foot of the driveway.

Darby tiptoed out of the high-fenced round pen

and closed the gate quietly behind her.

Why weren't the dogs barking? Maybe they'd gone into the bunkhouse with Kimo and they'd all settled down for an afternoon nap.

Dee was the one walking down the driveway and she started talking as soon as she saw Darby.

"Where's Cade?"

"He—" Darby exhaled loudly. Tutu knew best, and they'd tell Dee soon enough that her beloved pony was sick. "He's with Jonah, Kit, and everyone else, herding some horses up to Sky Mountain."

Dee's eyebrows arched high for an instant. Then she stared into the topmost branches of the nearby candlenut tree.

"I guess you're wondering why I'm hitchhiking out to visit Cade instead of going to work today." Dee got right to the point.

Darby wasn't wondering. Between them, Lisa Miller and Cricket had pretty much explained.

"Or maybe you already know," Dee went on. "Were you the one who got me fired?"

"I thought about it," Darby admitted, "but I didn't and now that I've talked to Tutu, I'm not sorry."

"Tutu? At least somebody around here isn't passing judgment on me."

"She remembers you from when you were a kid," Darby told her.

Dee's face softened as she smiled. "She does? Well, then she knows the kind of person I am, no matter what you might think."

Darby didn't know what to say, but they'd gone too far down this conversational road to stop now.

"It's written all over your face," Dee insisted. "I know you don't like me. You're a Kealoha. You all think you're better than everybody."

"That's not true!" Darby blurted, still trying to keep her voice low.

Dee waved her off with a flick of her wrist. "Sure it's not. Go get Cade for me, would ya?"

"I told you, he's out on a horse drive."

Dee scowled. "I thought you were making that up."

Darby shook her head.

"I'll just have a cigarette and then I'll head on over to my place. I want to check on Honi." She grinned a tight, joyless smile. "You wouldn't have an extra bale of hay for her, would you?"

She was going to have to say something soon, Darby thought. She found her shoulders shrugging almost as high as her earlobes as she tried to hide from the unpleasant announcement.

"You know we do," Darby said. "But, I think Tutu would like to see you, so, why don't you come up to the house when you're, um, done."

They both looked at the cigarette. "I am quitting these things," Dee insisted. "Tell Tutu I'll be there in just a minute."

Darby ran on ahead.

What are you afraid of? Darby asked herself. *Hurting*

her feelings like she's hurt Cade's a million times?

Darby toed off her boots and left them on the front porch.

She heard Tutu mixing things in the kitchen, but the first thing she said was, "Dee's here, is she?"

Darby nodded.

"And you haven't told her about Honi yet?"

Darby shook her head *no*.

"Since she'll be looking for another job, I've been thinking of getting her to help me on my rounds."

"But what if she keeps stealing, Tutu?"

Her great-grandmother looked up with a dreamy smile and said, "Ah, but what if she *doesn't?*"

This family gave second chances, Darby reminded herself.

Since she'd been given lots of them herself, she guessed it was fair to offer a couple to Cade's mother.

"Hey, Tutu!"

Darby jumped as Dee sauntered into the kitchen.

"Your great-granddaughter says you remember me from when I was a kid. I'm flattered. I sure remember you."

The warmth in Dee's voice startled Darby, and Tutu returned it.

"How are you, Dee?" Tutu asked.

Dee shook her flattened palm from side to side. "*Eh.* Not so great, to tell you the truth. I'm sure you've heard about Manny getting arrested. Having him gone is a blessing, but it's left me a little high and dry cashwise, if you know what I mean."

Darby was shocked at how honest Dee was being with Tutu and how quickly Tutu laid out her deal.

"So, I'd learn to be a nurse after all?" Dee asked.

Tutu nodded. "I'd do my best to teach you what I know," she said humbly.

"I could do that," Dee agreed, nodding. "I could really learn to be something worthwhile." Dee laughed as if she'd made a totally ridiculous statement, then added, "Might as well, since I've got nothing better to do."

Darby hoped her great-grandmother knew what she was getting into.

Tutu let Dee's acrid laughter hang in the kitchen for a moment before she spoke.

"Actually, your first patient is waiting, and I'm sorry to say—"

"Not Cade!" Dee pushed up from her lazy position leaning against the kitchen counter.

"No." Darby jumped in before Tutu could.

"Then—" Dee shook her head. Confused, she looked between Tutu and Darby. "Who?"

"It's Honi," Tutu said gently. "I'm afraid she's rather sick."

In minutes, Dee and Tutu were back in the round pen.

Dee dropped to her knees and stroked the pony's dusky mane.

"There's my baby," she crooned tenderly. "I missed you so much. Does my girl have a tummyache?"

Dee reached into the back pocket of her jeans and dug out a smashed bag of peppermint horse treats. Darby guessed they were probably filched from the feed store as a parting *gift* from Dee to Honi, but now wasn't the time to say so.

Honi's eyes opened wide, taking in Dee first and then the peppermint.

Dee held out a treat to the pony. Honi craned her neck forward, twitching her lips for it. Dee kept speaking soothingly to the pony, backing away inches at a time, moving just far enough out of reach to tantalize Honi.

The pony stretched.

Without waiting, Tutu threw her slight frame against Honi's haunches. Darby was about to join her when Honi struggled to her feet.

Dee rewarded her with the treat and quickly took out another bribe.

When Honi sidestepped unsteadily, almost falling, Dee's face contorted with worry. Her arms flashed out as if she'd catch the pony, and they came together.

It was amazing, Darby thought, how they helped each other regain their balance.

A lot can change in twenty-four hours, Darby thought. This time yesterday Honi could barely walk. Now, she trotted around her pen, insulted that she hadn't been included in the party that was in progress on the lanai above her.

Cricket had phoned with the news that the horses didn't have salmonella. Those at the Animal Rescue barn, and probably most of the humans and horses on the island, had been infected by waterborne bacteria that had given them what amounted to a two-day flu.

Even better, Cade and Dee were getting along and making plans, with Jonah's help. Tutu had allowed Kit to drive her back to her cottage on his way into town to see Medusa. And Cricket.

But Darby sat in the pastures below Sun House in the darkness and the rain, watching for her horse.

Before the sun had gone down, she'd tried calling Hoku to her by tightening her ponytail. It was their signal. Hoku had chosen it, and it had worked just two days ago.

Now Hoku chose to ignore it and Darby didn't blame her. Hoku couldn't understand that Darby had driven her out of her home for her own good.

Every muscle in Darby's body strained to keep her upright, though she could have lain down on the wet grass and slept.

Like shadowy ghost horses, the cremellos moved across the moonlit grass, but Hoku was nowhere in sight.

Don't be pupule, Jonah had told her. *She'll come to you.*

But the moon had traversed the black sky, trailing silver cloud skeins, and still Hoku didn't come to her.

And then she heard it.

The faint nicker that belonged only to Hoku made Darby stand.

It came again, and Darby began walking toward it. The sound of her boots swishing through the long grass covered other noises.

She stopped until the nicker came again, higher this time.

Darby held out her hands, hoping that even in the dark, her filly could see she carried no striking snake rope.

As the other horses parted for her, Darby walked through the broodmares and drowsy foals, threading her way between Cash and Judge, who'd discovered they had a lot in common as they grazed side by side.

And then, silvered by moonlight, Hoku stood alone before her. Waiting.

Darby didn't say a word. She listened to her filly's even breaths. Hoku wasn't a bit scared. She was teasing.

And even as Darby increased the tempo of her steps, bouncing on tiptoe toward her horse, then jogging, then running, Hoku waited.

Grab mane. Push off. Swing over.

The instant she was astride her wild sorrel filly, Hoku ducked her head, not to buck but to run under a low-hanging branch, carrying the human she trusted above all others into the night.

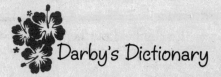

Darby's Dictionary

In case anybody reads this besides me, which it's too late to tell you not to do if you've gotten this far, I know this isn't a real dictionary. For one thing, it's not all correct, because I'm just adding things as I hear them. Besides, this dictionary is just to help me remember. Even though I'm pretty self-conscious about pronouncing Hawaiian words, it seems to me if I live here (and since I'm part Hawaiian), I should at least try to say things right.

ali'i — AH LEE EE — royalty, but it includes chiefs besides queens and kings and people like that

'aumakua — OW MA KOO AH — these are family guardians from ancient times. I think ancestors are supposed to come back and look out for their family members. Our *'aumakua* are owls and Megan's is a sea turtle.

<u>chicken skin</u> — goose bumps

<u>da kine</u> — DAH KYNE — "that sort of thing" or "stuff like that"

<u>hanai</u> — HA NYE E — a foster or adopted child, like Cade is Jonah's, but I don't know if it's permanent

<u>haole</u> — HOW LEE — a foreigner, especially a white person. I get called that, or *hapa* (half) haole, even though I'm part Hawaiian.

<u>hapa</u> — HA PAW — half

<u>hewa-hewa</u> — HEE VAH HEE VAH — crazy

<u>hiapo</u> — HIGH AH PO — a firstborn child, like me, and it's apparently tradition for grandparents, if they feel like it, to just take *hiapo* to raise!

<u>hoku</u> — HO COO — star

<u>holoholo</u> — HOE LOW HOW LOW — a pleasure trip that could be a walk, a ride, a sail, etc.

honu — HO NEW — sea turtle

ho'oponopono — HOE POE NO POE NO — this is a problem-solving process. It's sort of cool, because it's a native Hawaiian way of talking out problems.

'iolani — EE OH LAWN EE — this is a hawk that brings messages from the gods, but Jonah has it painted on his trucks as an owl bursting through the clouds

ipo — EE POE — sweetheart, actually short for *ku'uipo*

kanaka — KAH NAW KAH — man

kapu — KAH POO — forbidden, a taboo

keiki — KAY KEY — really, when I first heard this, I thought it sounded like a little cake! I usually hear it meaning a kid, or a child, but Megan says it can mean a calf or colt or almost any kind of young thing.

kupuna — COO POO NAW — an ancestor, but it can mean a grandparent too

lanai — LAH NA E — this is like a balcony or veranda. Sun House's is more like a long balcony with a view of the pastures.

<u>lau hala</u> — LA OO HA LA — some kind of leaf in shades of brown, used to make paniolo hats like Cade's. I guess they're really expensive.

<u>lei</u> — LAY E — necklace of flowers. I thought they were pronounced LAY, but Hawaiians add another sound. I also thought leis were sappy touristy things, but getting one is a real honor, from the right people.

<u>lei niho palaoa</u> — LAY NEEHO PAH LAHOAH — necklace made for old-time Hawaiian royalty from braids of their own hair. It's totally *kapu*—forbidden— for anyone else to wear it.

<u>luna</u> — LOU NUH — a boss or top guy, like Jonah's stallion

<u>mahalo</u> — MAW HA LOW — thank you

<u>malihini</u> — MUH LEE HEE NEE — stranger or newcomer

<u>menehune</u> — MEN AY WHO NAY — little people

<u>ohia</u> — OH HE UH — a tree like the one next to Hoku's corral

<u>pali</u> — PAW LEE — cliffs

paniolo — PAW NEE OH LOW — cowboy or cow-girl

pau — POW — finished, like Kimo is always asking, "You *pau*?" to see if I'm done working with Hoku or shoveling up after the horses

Pele — PAY LAY — the volcano goddess. Red is her color. She's destructive with fire, but creative because she molds lava into new land. She's easily offended if you mess with things sacred to her, like the ohia tree, lehua flowers, 'ohelo berries, and the wild horse herd on Two Sisters.

pueo — POO AY OH — an owl, our family guardian. The very coolest thing is that one lives in the tree next to Hoku's corral.

pupule — POO POO LAY — crazy

tutu — TOO TOO — great-grandmother

wahine — WAH HE NEE — a lady (or women)

 Darby's Diary

<u>Ellen Kealoha Carter</u>—my mom, and since she's responsible for me being in Hawaii, I'm putting her first. Also, I miss her. My mom is a beautiful and talented actress, but she hasn't had her big break yet. Her job in Tahiti might be it, which is sort of ironic because she's playing a Hawaiian for the first time and she swore she'd never return to Hawaii. And here I am. I get the feeling she had huge fights with her dad, Jonah, but she doesn't hate Hawaii.

<u>Cade</u>—fifteen or so, he's Jonah's adopted son. Jonah's been teaching him all about being a paniolo. I thought he was Hawaiian, but when he took off his hat he had blond hair—in a braid! Like old-time vaqueros—

weird! He doesn't go to school, just takes his classes by correspondence through the mail. He wears this poncho that's almost black it's such a dark green, and he blends in with the forest. Kind of creepy the way he just appears out there. Not counting Kit, Cade might be the best rider on the ranch.

Hoku kicked him in the chest. I wish she hadn't. He told me that his stepfather beat him all the time.

Cathy Kato—forty or so? She's the ranch manager and, really, the only one who seems to manage Jonah. She's Megan's mom and the widow of a paniolo, Ben. She has messy blond-brown hair to her chin, and she's a good cook, but she doesn't think so. It's like she's just pulling herself back together after Ben's death.

I get the feeling she used to do something with advertising or public relations on the mainland.

Jonah Kaniela Kealoha—my grandfather could fill this whole notebook. Basically, though, he's harsh/nice, serious/funny, full of legends and stories about magic, but real down-to-earth. He's amazing with horses, which is why they call him the Horse Charmer. He's not that tall, maybe 5'8", with black hair that's getting gray, and one of his fingers is still kinked where it was broken by a teacher because he spoke Hawaiian in class! I don't like his "don't touch the horses unless they're working for you" theory, but it totally works. I need to figure out why.

Kimo—he's so nice! I guess he's about twenty-five, Hawaiian, and he's just this sturdy, square, friendly guy. He drives in every morning from his house over by Crimson Vale, and even though he's late a lot, I've never seen anyone work so hard.

Kit Ely—the ranch foreman, the boss, next to Jonah. He's Sam's friend Jake's brother and a real buckaroo. He's about 5'10" with black hair. He's half Shoshone, but he could be mistaken for Hawaiian, if he wasn't always promising to whip up a batch of Nevada chili and stuff like that. And he wears a totally un-Hawaiian leather string with brown-streaked turquoise stones around his neck. He got to be foreman through his rodeo friend Pani (Ben's buddy). Kit's left wrist got pulverized in a rodeo fall. He's still amazing with horses, though.

Cricket—is Kit's girlfriend! Her hair's usually up in a messy bun and she wears glasses. She drives a ratty Jeep and said, to his face, "I'm nobody's girl, Ely." He just laughed. She works at the feed store and is an expert for the Animal Rescue Society in Hapuna.

Megan Kato—Cathy's fifteen-year-old daughter, a super athlete with long reddish-black hair. She's beautiful and popular and I doubt she'd be my friend if we just met at school. Maybe, though, because she's nice at heart. She half makes fun of Hawaiian legends, then turns around and acts really serious about them. Her Hawaiian name is Mekana.

The Zinks—they live on the land next to Jonah. Their name doesn't sound Hawaiian, but that's all I know.

Wow, I met Patrick and now I know lots more about the Zinks. Like, the rain forest—the part where Tutu told me not to go—used to be part of the A-Z (Acosta and Zink!) sugar plantation and it had a village and factory and train tracks. But in 1890, when it was going strong, people didn't care that much about the environment, and they really wrecked it, so now Patrick's parents are trying to let the forest take it back over. They hope it will go back to the way it was before people got there. I still don't know his parents' names, but I think Patrick said his dad mostly fishes and his mom is writing a history of the old plantation.

Oh, and that part Tutu said about the old sugar plantation being kind of dangerous? It REALLY is!

Patrick Zink—is geeky, super-smart, and seriously accident-prone. He looks a little like Harry Potter would if he wore Band-Aids and Ace bandages and had skinned knees and elbows. He says he was born for adventure and knows all about the rain forest and loves Mistwalker, his horse. He's not into his family being rich, just feels like they have a lot to pay back to the island for what their family's old sugar cane plantation did to it environmentally. He likes it (and so do I!) that they're letting the rain forest reclaim it.

Tutu—my great-grandmother. She lives out in the rain forest like a medicine woman or something, and she looks like my mom will when she's old. She has a pet owl.

Aunt Babe Borden—Jonah's sister, so she's really my great-aunt. She owns half of the family land, which is divided by a border that runs between the Two Sisters. Aunt Babe and Jonah don't get along, and though she's fashionable and caters to rich people at her resort, she and her brother are identically stubborn. Aunt Babe pretends to be all business, but she loves her cremello horses and I think she likes having me and Hoku around.

Duxelles Borden—if you lined up all the people on Hawaii and asked me to pick out one NOT related to me, it would be Duxelles, but it turns out she's my cousin. Tall (I come up to her shoulders), strong, and with this metallic blond hair, she's popular despite being a bully. She lives with Aunt Babe while her mom travels with her dad, who's a world-class kayaker. About the only thing Duxelles and I have in common is we're both swimmers. Oh, and I gave her a nickname—Duckie.

<u>Potter family</u>—Ann, plus her two little brothers, Toby and Buck, their parents, Ramona and Ed, and lots of horses for their riding therapy program. I like them all. Sugarfoot scares me a little, though.

<u>Manny</u>—Cade's Hawaiian stepfather pretends to be a taro farmer in Crimson Vale, but he sells ancient artifacts from the caves, and takes shots at wild horses. When Cade was little, Manny used him to rob caves and beat him up whenever he felt like it.

<u>Dee</u>—Cade's mom. She's tall and strong-looking (with blond hair like his), but too weak to keep Manny from beating Cade. Her slogan must be "You don't know what it's like to be a single mom," because Cade repeats it every time he talks about her. My mom's single and she'd never let anyone break my jaw!

<u>Tyson</u>—this kid in my Ecology class who wears a hooded gray sweatshirt all the time, like he's hiding his identity and he should. He's a sarcastic bully. All he's really done to me personally is call me a haole crab (really rude) and warn me against saying anything bad about Pele. Like I would! But I've heard rumors that he mugs tourists when they go "off-limits." Really, he acts like HIS culture (anything Hawaiian) is off-limits to everyone but him.

<u>Shan Stonerow</u>—according to Sam Forster, he once

owned Hoku and his way of training horses was to "show them who's boss."

<u>My teachers</u>—
Mr. Silva—with his lab coat and long gray hair, he looks like he should teach wizardry instead of Ecology
Miss Day—my English and P.E. teacher. She is great, understanding, smart, and I have no idea how she tolerates team-teaching with Coach R.
Mrs. Martindale—my Creative Writing teacher is not as much of a witch as some people think.
Coach Roffmore—stocky with a gray crew cut, he was probably an athlete when he was young, but now he just has a rough attitude. Except to his star swimmer, my sweet cousin Duckie. I have him for Algebra and P.E., and he bugs me to be on the swim team.

❧ ANIMALS! ❧

<u>Hoku</u>—my wonderful sorrel filly! She's about two and a half years old, a full sister to the Phantom, and boy, does she show it! She's fierce (hates men) but smart, and a one-girl (ME!) horse for sure. She is definitely a herd girl, and when it comes to choosing between me and other horses, it's a real toss-up. Not that I blame her. She's run free for a long time, and I don't want to take away what makes her special.

She loves hay, but she's really HEAD-SHY due to Shan Stonerow's early "training," which, according to

Sam, was beating her.

Hoku means "star." Her dam is Princess Kitty, but her sire is a mustang named Smoke and he's mustang all the way back to a "white renegade with murder in his eye" (Mrs. Allen).

Navigator—my riding horse is a big, heavy Quarter Horse that reminds me of a knight's charger. He has Three Bars breeding (that's a big deal), but when he picked me, Jonah let him keep me! He's black with rusty rings around his eyes and a rusty muzzle. (Even though he looks black, the proper description is brown, they tell me.) He can find his way home from any place on the island. He's sweet, but no pushover. Just when I think he's sort of a safety net for my beginning riding skills, he tests me.

Joker—Cade's Appaloosa gelding is gray splattered with black spots and has a black mane and tail. He climbs like a mountain goat and always looks like he's having a good time. I think he and Cade have a history; maybe Jonah took them in together?

Biscuit—buckskin gelding, one of Ben's horses, a dependable cow pony. Kit rides him a lot.

Hula Girl—chestnut cutter

Blue Ginger—blue roan mare with tan foal

Honolulu Lulu—bay mare

Tail Afire (Koko)—fudge-brown mare with silver mane and tail

Blue Moon—Blue Ginger's baby

Moonfire—Tail Afire's baby

Black Cat—Lady Wong's black foal

Luna Dancer—Hula Girl's bay baby

Honolulu Half Moon

Conch—grulla cow pony, gelding, needs work. Megan rides him sometimes.

Kona—big gray, Jonah's cow horse

Luna—beautiful, full-maned bay stallion is king of 'Iolani Ranch. He and Jonah seem to have a bond.

Lady Wong—dappled gray mare and Kona's dam. Her current foal is Black Cat.

Australian shepherds—pack of five: Bart, Jack, Jill, Peach, and Sass

Pipsqueak/Pip—little shaggy white dog that runs with the big dogs, belongs to Megan and Cathy

Pigolo—an orphan (piglet) from the storm

Francie—the fainting goat

Tango—Megan's once-wild rose roan mare. I think she and Hoku are going to be pals.

Sugarfoot—Ann Potter's horse is a beautiful Morab (half Morgan and half Arabian, she told me). He's a caramel-and-white paint with one white foot. He can't be used with "clients" at the Potters' because he's a chaser. Though Ann and her mother, Ramona, have pretty much schooled it out of him, he's still not quite trustworthy. If he ever chases me, I'm supposed to stand my ground, whoop, and holler. Hope I never have to do it!

Flight—this cremello mare belongs to Aunt Babe (she has a whole herd of cremellos) and nearly died of longing for her foal. She was a totally different horse—beautiful and spirited—once she got him back!

Stormbird—Flight's cream-colored (with a blush of palomino) foal with turquoise eyes has had an exciting life for a four-month-old. He's been shipwrecked, washed ashore, fended for himself, and rescued.

<u>Medusa</u>—Black Lava's lead mare—with the heart of a lion—just might be Kit's new horse.

<u>Black Lava</u>—stallion from Crimson Vale, and the wildest thing I've ever seen in my life! He just vibrates with it. He's always showing his teeth, flashing his eyes (one brown and one blue), rearing, and usually thorns and twigs are snarled in his mane and tail. He killed Kanaka Luna's sire and Jonah almost shot him for it. He gave him a second chance by cutting an X on the bottom of Black Lava's hoof wall, so he'd know if he came around again. Wouldn't you know he likes Hoku?

<u>Soda</u>—Ann's blue-black horse. Unlike Sugarfoot, he's a good therapy horse when he's had enough exercise.

<u>Buckin' Baxter</u>—blue roan in training as a cow horse and I can stay on him!

<u>Prettypaint</u>—used to be my mom's horse, but now she lives with Tutu. She's pale gray with bluish spots on her heels, and silky feathers on her fetlocks. She kneels for Tutu to get on and off, not like she's doing a trick, but as if she's carrying a queen.

<u>Mistwalker</u>—is Patrick's horse. She's a beautiful black-and-white paint—bred by Jonah! He could hardly stand to admit she was born on 'Iolani Ranch, which is silly. Her conformation is almost pure Quarter Horse

and you can see that beyond her coloring. And what he doesn't know about Mistwalker's grandfather (probably) won't hurt him!

Honi—Cade's mom's gray pony. Her name means "kiss" and she really does kiss. Cade jokes that his mom likes Honi best. He also says Honi is "half Arab and half Welsh and all bossy." And, she likes to eat water lilies!

❧ PLACES ❧

Lehua High School—the school Megan and I go to. School colors are red and gold.

Crimson Vale—it's an amazing and magical place, and once I learn my way around, I bet I'll love it. It's like a maze, though. Here's what I know: From town you can go through the valley or take the ridge road—valley has lily pads, waterfalls, wild horses, and rainbows. The ridge route (Pali?) has sweeping turns that almost made me sick. There are black rock teeter-totter-looking things that are really ancient altars and a SUDDEN drop-off down to a white sand beach. Hawaiian royalty are supposedly buried in the cliffs.

Moku Lio Hihiu—Wild Horse Island, of course!

Sky Mountain—goes up to five thousand feet, sometimes snow-capped, sometimes called Mountain to the Sky by most of the older folks, and it's supposed to be the home of a white stallion named Snowfire.

<u>Two Sisters</u>—cone-shaped "mountains"—a borderline between them divides Babe's land from Jonah's, one of them is an active volcano.

<u>Sun House</u>—our family place. They call it plantation style, but it's like a sugar plantation, not a Southern mansion. It has an incredible lanai that overlooks pastures all the way to Mountain to the Sky and Two Sisters. Upstairs is this little apartment Jonah built for my mom, but she's never lived in it.

<u>Hapuna</u>—biggest town on island, has airport, flagpole, public and private schools, etc., palm trees, and coconut trees

<u>'Iolani Ranch</u>—our home ranch. 2,000 acres, the most beautiful place in the world.

<u>Pigtail Fault</u>—near the active volcano. It looks more like a steam vent to me, but I'm no expert. According to Cade, it got its name because a poor wild pig ended up head down in it and all you could see was his tail. Too sad!

<u>Sugar Sands Cove Resort</u>—Aunt Babe and her polo-

player husband, Phillipe, own this resort on the island. It has sparkling white buildings and beaches and a four-star hotel. The most important thing to me is that Sugar Sands Cove Resort has the perfect water-schooling beach for me and Hoku.

The Old Sugar Plantation—Tutu says it's a dangerous place. Really, it's just the ruins of A-Z sugar plantation, half of which belonged to Patrick's family. Now it's mostly covered with moss and vines and ferns, but you can still see what used to be train tracks, some stone steps leading nowhere, a chimney, and rickety wooden structures which are hard to identify.

❧ ON THE RANCH, THERE ARE ❧
PASTURES WITH NAMES LIKE:

Sugar Mill and Upper Sugar Mill—for cattle

Two Sisters—for young horses, one- and two-year-olds they pretty much leave alone

Flatland—mares and foals

Pearl Pasture—borders the rain forest, mostly two- and three-year-olds in training

Borderlands—saddle herd and Luna's compound

I guess I should also add me . . .

<u>Darby Leilani Kealoha Carter</u>—I love horses more than anything, but books come in second. I'm thirteen, and one-quarter Hawaiian, with blue eyes and black hair down to about the middle of my back. On a good day, my hair is my best feature. I'm still kind of skinny, but I don't look as sickly as I did before I moved here. I think Hawaii's curing my asthma. Fingers crossed.

I have no idea what I did to land on Wild Horse Island, but I want to stay here forever.

DARBY'S GENEALOGY

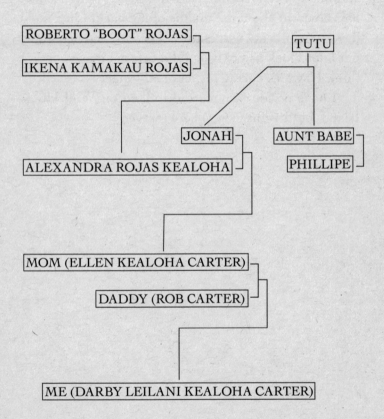

ROBERTO "BOOT" ROJAS

IKENA KAMAKAU ROJAS

TUTU

JONAH

AUNT BABE

PHILLIPE

ALEXANDRA ROJAS KEALOHA

MOM (ELLEN KEALOHA CARTER)

DADDY (ROB CARTER)

ME (DARBY LEILANI KEALOHA CARTER)

Darby and Hoku's adventures continue in ...

SNOWFIRE

 Snowfire

Darby Carter pressed her legs against her stirrup leathers. The blue roan gelding beneath her stepped out into a jog, just as she'd asked, but the herd of red cattle ahead of her didn't speed up. They scattered.

Ten cows and eight calves didn't amount to a stampede, but Darby loosened her reins, letting Baxter extend his trot. His sudden speed made her black ponytail snap, but the cattle ignored the horse and rider.

"Get back!" Darby raised her right hand from her reins.

Her job was to watch for stragglers, but Cade hadn't told her the cattle might spread out and stray in all different directions.

She shot a look up at Cade. The young Hawaiian cowboy rode on Hula Girl, a chestnut cutter, at the front of the herd with his hala hat pulled down, almost covering his short, tight braid. He made this chore look easy. If he knew she was entirely messing up her part of moving the cattle to higher pastures, he didn't show it.

Forget riding loose and relaxed, Darby thought. The only way she could keep the cattle moving forward was by speeding closer to the animals.

Baxter was new at this, but Darby didn't blame the gelding for their awkwardness. Baxter's blueberries-and-cream-colored coat was dark with sweat as he tried to do what she wanted.

Baxter's ears swiveled. He snorted with excitement as a calf corkscrewed its skinny tail, then straightened it high in the air before bounding away from the herd.

"Oh, no, you don't," Darby scolded.

The calf actually looked back at her before giving a buck of high spirits. Then he ran.

Should she desert her position at the back of the herd to pursue the calf?

Baxter flattened his ears and decided for her. As he bolted after the calf, hooves falling in the same dusty, zigzag path, Darby crowded against the gelding's neck.

Baxter was so excited, he raced right past the calf. Darby turned him back, trying to block the fugitive calf's escape. Baxter obeyed, making such a tight arc,

Darby's left stirrup skidded on dirt.

It wasn't pretty, but it worked. The calf gave a frightened bawl, then ran back to his mother.

Darby gave Baxter's sweaty neck a pat, but the gelding didn't notice. Once more, he was watching the herd.

The cattle mooed, rolled their eyes, and a few stopped. Others swung their big bodies back toward the ranch.

If the cattle made it back to where they'd started, Darby knew her grandfather, Jonah, and Kimo, a hardworking ranch hand, would turn her lack of skill into a good-natured joke.

What was she doing wrong? She was about to shout her question at Cade when Hula Girl slowed. Leaving the lead to a loud red cow, Cade made his mount drop back along the right side of the herd until she matched steps with Baxter.

"Slow and easy," Cade told Darby. "And quiet."

Hula Girl's gait dropped down to a walk, so Darby slowed Baxter.

Amazingly, the cattle moved back into a calm herd and continued their journey toward Upper Sugar Mill pasture. They walked with purpose, swinging their heads at occasional flies, but they looked relaxed, and Darby couldn't figure out why.

"Don't believe the movies," Cade's voice was so low, Darby strained to hear him.

"Don't believe the movies?" she repeated.

"You could make this herd do what you want them to do by sitting over there"—he nodded toward a cinnamon-colored mudslide on a green hill at least a mile away—"and raising your hand."

Maybe you could, Darby thought, but she just said, "Okay."

Darby watched Cade ride on back to the head of the herd, and muffled a cough with her hand. It wasn't her asthma kicking up, just a reaction to the dust, but she was reassured by the feel of her inhaler in her front pocket.

Since she'd come to 'Iolani Ranch three months ago, her asthma had practically disappeared. The clean ocean air on Moku Lio Hihiu—Hawaiian for Wild Horse Island—was a huge improvement over the pollution and smog of Pacific Pinnacles, California.

Even to herself, she'd stopped calling California home.

Surrounded by flowers and birdsong, Darby drifted into thoughts of how much she loved Hawaii, how convinced she was that she'd landed in exactly the right place in the world. How many other eighth graders were riding up a tropical mountainside during their study breaks?

As a first-year student at Lehua High School, this was the first time she'd faced two-hour-long final exams. She'd had her last full day of classes yesterday, and today she'd gotten off at noon. Tomorrow finals began.

When Baxter tried to lope up the hill, Darby tightened her reins and kept him at a walk.

"To save your legs," she muttered to the gelding, but that wasn't the only reason. Baxter had to know what was expected of him. She couldn't just be along for the ride.

When they finally reached the entrance to Upper Sugar Mill pasture, Darby smiled. The cattle milled impatiently. They'd recognized the place and bumped against the fence, eager to get inside and sample the fresh pasture.

Darby lifted her shoulder to let her T-shirt blot a drop of sweat that had trailed down her cheek, then sighed and sat back against her saddle cantle. They'd made it.

Cade swung Hula Girl alongside the gate and slid the bolt, opening it from the saddle. Then he nodded.

Darby hesitated at his signal, and Cade said, "Take 'em on in."

With Baxter at a flat-footed walk behind them, the cattle shoved through the opening.

Wide spans of grass rolled over mounds of earth and down slopes, rising and falling in search of the horizon where the Two Sisters volcanoes wore leis of cloud.

Beyond, the grass turned dark emerald as it surrounded Sky Mountain. Today the farthest peak looked like an upside-down golden cone topped with vanilla ice cream.

The cattle had just fanned out and fallen to grazing when Jack and Jill, two of the ranch's five Australian shepherds, trotted over a hill crest.

Kit must be somewhere nearby, Darby thought, and then, she noticed how quietly the dogs approached. Even though their mouths widened in canine grins, they didn't agitate the cattle.

"Steady," Cade told the dogs, and the two let their alert ears fall as they trailed behind Hula Girl and did their best to take no notice of the cattle.

Cade rode around to Darby's side and nodded.

The movement could have meant "nice job," or "not bad." Cade's compliments were rare. The only thing Darby was sure he didn't mean by the nod was "give me your horse and walk home."

Instead of gushing her thanks, Darby returned his nod and, once more, congratulated her horse.

"You're just as 'cowy' as Jonah thought," she said, and gave Baxter's withers a little massage.

"Not bad," Cade agreed, but just as Darby's spirits soared, he added, "At least it wasn't a full-blown wreck."

In cattlemen's terms, a wreck could be a stampede, a fall from a horse, anything unplanned and disastrous, and even though Cade had said the herd's response to her herding *hadn't* been a wreck, Darby winced.

"You stay relaxed and he'll get the hang of it soon," Cade said. "More practice and you two'll make a team."

"Good," Darby said, but it wasn't Baxter she worried about.

The horse had been bred for cow sense. She hadn't, and she had a lot to learn.

"When you know what you're doing, he'll feel it," Cade said. "Baxter's a fast learner."

"It's not him I'm worried about," Darby said.

According to her grandfather she was a natural rider, but she was still making mistakes. Here on 'Iolani Ranch, that was okay, but biting the dust in front of crowded stands at a rodeo was something else.

And that was what she was practicing for: a real rodeo. She'd agreed to compete on Baxter in the *keiki*—Hawaiian for "kids"—ranch rodeo.

Discover all the adventures on
Wild Horse Island!